THE FIRE BETWEEN US

Candace S. Gwynn

This is a work of fiction. All of the characters, organizations, and events portrayed in this novel are either products of the author's imagination or are used fictitiously.

THE FIRE BETWEEN US

Copyright © 2025 Candace Sharpe-Gwynn

All rights reserved.

No portion of this book may be reproduced in any form without written permission from the author, except as permitted by U.S. copyright law.

ISBN: 979-8-218-85379-2

Dedication

For Patricia A. Francis,
You saw past a frustrated, dyslexic, quiet little girl and saw the poet she could become. I still remember our first trip to the Havre de Grace library in 1987. School had just let out for the summer. That day, you told me, "Books can be a vacation; just take your time, and you can get to anywhere you want to go." That day, I checked out *Sink or Swim by Betty Miles,* and I never stopped reading. This moment showed me how to push past my limitations. You didn't just tell me I could do anything; you encouraged it. So, though you aren't here to witness this moment. This moment doesn't happen without you. Thank you for believing in me.

Prologue

Heat forged its way before any inkling of a flicker. There was no light, no warning, just the acrid smell of cedar and spice burning. Memories turning to ash. The woman jolted awake, her skin already slick with sweat from the rising temperature. Crackles spoken in whispers. A language only the oldest soul remembered. Followed by smoke crouching below the windowpane, gray tendrils reaching like desperate fingers. The smoke tasted of copper and revenge on her tongue as it stalked through the hallway. This was no accident; it was summoned.

And now, blood was demanded.

She heard its primal screams. Chants from a dead language.

It had returned.

For weeks, she had warned her son that his actions would be their certain demise. He wanted only to protect them. At least that's what she told herself as she watched him grow more reckless and more desperate. Some deals, however, were simply not meant to happen. Arrogantly refusing to take heed, he unknowingly obtained a relic meant for death, not safety. This relic, which he intended to sell, compelled him to claim its power as his own. Now that the deal was done, it was the children's lives that the fire came to collect.

She scurried to the closet. Her hands were shaking as she pried up the loose floorboards, revealing the cedar box hidden inside. Her family had the responsibility of guarding the contents, a task she'd almost abandoned.

She had placed the box in the floorboard, hoping that the old ways would be forgotten along with it.

She opened the box with trembling hands and pulled out what would now be her only hope. A quilt. Red as fresh blood, with black thread and golden embroidery sewn into the seams. It pulsed in her hands like a heartbeat, warming her palms and fingertips, alive with an ancient power that made the air around it shimmer. "For escape," she whispered to it, the old words coming back to her tongue like muscle memory.

It listened.

In the chaos, she only attempted to grab a few items before she ran to her twin grandsons, awakening them in a rush. She wrapped the glowing fabric around them. Then, they, three, wrapped in a faint shimmer, like embers glowing under ash, moved boldly through the inferno. Hungry flames that had devoured their home curled back as they advanced, leaving a corridor of breathable air where blistering heat should have seared their lungs.

The fire's retreat was not in fear, but in recognition. It bowed, watched, and obeyed. With smoke in her lungs, tears in her heart, and grief in her bones, she followed the heatless path the fabric revealed. Flames parted like curtains as they escaped through the wreckage of betrayal, untouched.

Behind her, the fire howled at their absence.

It would remember.

And so would she.

They emerged on the other side, gasping for air, and she didn't look back. There was no way to repay what had been taken from her. She looked down at the boy on her left, Ali, his eyes pale gray like hers. He was much like her, a reminder of her people, her past. She retrieved from her pocket the only two objects she saved from the fire. On Ali's right arm, she placed a bracelet that belonged to her mother. "Protector." She smiled.

The other boy, Eli. His eyes, an intriguing shade of hazel.

Like his grandfather before him. The late husband she lost years before the fire they just escaped. This boy would now be her future. She placed a crescent moon necklace belonging to his grandfather, forged from bone. "Power." She gripped his chin, showing him how to hold his head up high. She wrapped the quilt around her shoulders and led the boys to safer ground.

This was her bloodline and the last magic her family had promised to protect.

By morning, they would journey west. Toward the ocean. Toward America. To start again.

1

KINDLING HEARTS
(Yah-Yah)

The vision hit like a slap.

Flames, choking smoke, the feeling of being hunted.

I jolted awake, hand flying to my throat as phantom heat crawled up my neck. The dream clung to me like ash, refusing to shake loose even as the gray morning crept through my curtains.

Just a dream, I told myself, but my pulse was hammering against my ribs like my heart knew better.

I sat up slowly.

I had been having the same nightmare for weeks.

There was always the fire. There was always a sense that something was hunting, that something was coming.

My aunt says that dreams carry messages, but she's so damn cryptic, sometimes understanding her can be an impossible task.

I stared into the surrounding space.

My alarm hadn't gone off, but there was no point in trying to go back to sleep; I had tossed and turned with restless energy for most of the night. I've been carrying around this nerve-racking but familiar feeling.

A feeling that something's shifting in the world around me.

Past trauma has made me constantly vigilant. I am always on the lookout for danger. After all, Titi raised me to trust my instincts, and so far, that has never led me wrong.

I dragged myself out of bed and headed to my bedroom window, pulling back the curtains and revealing the street spread out below me.

A neighborhood lined with perfectly pruned trees as antique as the Victorian facades and wrought iron fences that stood behind them.

This was Royal Hills.

Living in a place like this was what I had always dreamed of.

Back then, I was a scrawny little girl living with my aunt, uprooted from everything I'd ever known.

Five miles south of here is the Far Side of Nevermore, the place I was born.

The place that circumstance allowed me to escape.

Unharmed.

Though not without scars, and not with my mom and dad.

Sometimes I could almost forget that the entire other world existed.

But not today.

Today, it felt way too close. Like if I reached out my arm, I could touch it.

Hold it.

I have a sense of doom clinging to me like a passenger.

Fine.

It could ride along. But I would not be stuck here with it

I had to get out of this house.

Now, twenty minutes later, I slip into the backseat of a black Honda Accord, hoping the driver will respect my obvious need for complete silence. The silence I had requested through the app that sent him.

No such luck.

"You from around here?" he started before we'd even pulled away from the curb.

I kept my eyes focused on my phone. "Mmm hmm." Oh Lord, I could tell more was coming.

"This is a good place to live," he continued. "Drugs and corruption have taken over many of the neighborhoods that surround this place. But right here has good people, not a lot of riffraff. No?"

At that, I cringed.

Clenching my jaw.

I knew exactly what he meant by *riffraff*.

He meant people like me.

People from neighborhoods like where I once lived.

"Nope, no *riffraff* at all," I managed.

Trying not to be offended and looking for a way to disconnect immediately.

The mention of the drugs taking over hit me like ice water. I turned toward the window, watching Royal Hills as it blurred past.

Now all I could feel was the old familiar ache settling in my chest.

Trauma.

After the hurt heals, you're still reminded of it by the scars left behind.

Devil Haze.

Even thinking of the name made my throat tight.

Most people in neighborhoods like this one saw it as just another drug problem, something that happened to other people in other families.

Other places.

Not here.

But a different understanding raised me.

We learn that this destruction had been deliberate, calculated.

The decay of drugs and corruption had been a weapon aimed at our communities.

Communities that had grown too strong, too independent.

I pressed my forehead against the cool glass. The sky above seemed to mock my mood, dreary, sullen, almost fed up, even, but refusing to succumb to the pending rain. The driver just kept on talking, but his voice faded as memories I spent years burying desperately clawed their way to the surface.

My mother in her last months was so frail, her eyes vacant, glassy. Her skin, ashen, almost gray. My dad's desperate attempts to get her clean had been unsuccessful. I watched him cry endlessly through the night. Saw him begging her desperately to come back to us.

The nights my mother roamed the streets alone. My father would stay waiting for her to return. Often I witnessed him just staring into space, lost without her.

Speechless, almost lifeless.

I was six when it all ended.

When he had had enough, my father decided the only way out was to take her with him. Into whatever came after, without me.

My aunt Titi uprooted her life to come raise me. Although she could never explain why some families separated while others remained together, living happily ever after. She could prove that no matter what trouble life intended to bring, she and I would face it together. My aunt taught me to fight to the very end, even if some fights are rigged from the beginning.

Yes, my disdain for Haze is personal; it has taken away everything I have ever known.

Now, this literal ride down memory lane, for me, could not end soon enough.

"Can you drop me off at the cafe?" I said so suddenly that I surprised myself.

The Rowhouse Roast.

One of my favorite places.

Daylight creeps through the tall windows, casting golden rectangles that stretch across the polished wood floors, highlighting the worn grooves where countless footsteps trace familiar paths.

Shadows from wrought-iron window frames create delicate geometric patterns on the weathered brick walls.

Jazz crackles softly through the speakers. A moody saxophone sliding between chopped piano loops. Like a city soundtrack, playing on worn-out vinyl. Seamlessly mixed with the rhythmic whirr and hiss of a chrome espresso machine, like a DJ blended it in.

The gentle clinking of dishes created a cozy mixtape of sounds.

The rich smell of fresh coffee filled the space, layered with hints of cinnamon and vanilla from the pastry case.

The worn leather of the vintage armchairs added a lived-in warmth, grounding the place in quiet comfort.

At the register, a crooked chalkboard menu listed seasonal drinks in bright, loopy handwriting. Behind the counter, their movements were smooth and practiced, like second nature.

I ordered a tall caramel macchiato with a double shot and extra whipped cream. Something sweet and strong to take the edge off.

I choose my regular seat at the table in the far corner, surrounded by the quiet rustle of turning pages from dog-eared novels and newspapers. Comforted by the urgent staccato of fingers frantically tapping on laptop keyboards as students and writers lost themselves in their work.

Conversations at nearby tables filled the air with fragments of laughter, whispered discussions, and the occasional clink of a coffee cup being set down with quiet satisfaction.

The local news somberly played on a television mounted on the other side of the room. Hesitantly, I looked towards the screen.

Breaking News.

Reports of another young girl missing flashed across the screen.

I paused.

A chill moved swiftly across my skin, sharp and sudden, like someone had jerked open a window.

I was staring at her photo on the screen when the coffee in my mouth turned sour. The feeling hit me hard, strange, and uneasy. It resembled recognition.

Then, with my eyes closed.

In a flash, I saw a pair of innocent eyes.

Hers.

She was curled in a dark corner, scared, alone, trembling.

I was there with her, breathing the stale air, bending low to see her, to comfort her.

Then I reached into my pocket and handed her something, a mirror, small, strange and glimmering in the dark.

Then, without warning, the surrounding walls vanished in smoke.

With a gasp, I came to my senses. "The fuck?" I questioned through a faint fog of confusion. "You don't even know that girl."

So why was my stomach twisted?

It was like my body was trying to tell me something, but I couldn't keep up.

I was so tired I could barely function.

It was at that moment my sky, dreary, sullen, and fed up, released a single drop of rain that was now traveling slowly down my cheek.

After wiping my face with the back of my hand, I take a massive gulp of my double-shot espresso blended with a super-dose of reality.

I couldn't imagine the pain placed on five separate families.

I forced my eyes away from the screen. "Pull it together, Yah," I said, attempting to jolt myself back to reality.

The vibration of my cell startled me.

7:30AM

Sky:

Good mornin girlie? Wya?

Relieved that it wasn't exactly bad news. My best friend always seemed to check in at the right moment.

* * *

7

Me:
Hey girl, made a pit-stop.
Headed to work in a few

Back to life, back to reality.

Now I was checking my salon schedule on my phone, getting in the proper mental space for today's appointments.

It felt like a lot to tackle before I could finally get back home and relax, maybe binge a sci-fi series, watch a silly rom-com, or settle for a bourbon-induced coma.

Desperately, I tried to shake it off.

I started gathering my things: phone, keys, my day planner, moving quickly, ready to press on. I was reaching for my half-empty cup.

Then I saw him.

I froze mid-reach, my breath tangled in my throat.

Standing at the entrance, he looked like he had just stepped out of a dream I wasn't ready to wake from. His eyes scanned the room with quiet intent. My breath stopped.

The usual noise in my head dulled, like someone had turned the volume down on the world.

Naturally, the first thing I noticed was his hair, auburn locs hanging below his shoulders. His muscular frame towered over me at 6'2". He had an unreal beauty, the kind you swear only lives in myth or high-fashion spreads.

But he was real, and he glowed. His hazel eyes appeared to resemble a piercing golden light, and I melted from the inside.

Unknowingly, I studied every detail, from the black V-neck that revealed every muscle striation it clung to, to the ivory crescent moon that hung on a braided golden rope just below his collarbone. He wore slightly faded blue jeans, not too baggy but not too tight, and not a single wrinkle present. And maybe he was walking, but as I saw it, he was gliding towards the register in a pair of black casual oxfords, size 12.

I melted.

The embers inside me wouldn't dare threaten to dwindle.

Then I smelled him.

My hips adjusted to the sensation of his presence as I floated in the scent he left behind. Amber and oud wrapping around me like silk.

I licked my lips, and I could taste him…shit.

Pure instinct was propelling me to stand and go to him.

My head said, "What are you doing, Yah? You don't even know this man. Just sit back down!"

But my gut?

My gut was already on the move.

Titi always told me, "If you feel it in your gut, you damn well better listen." And right now, my whole body was talking to me.

Before I could talk myself out of it, I stood. Legs shaky, pulse racing.

Each step across the cafe felt like the universe was watching. Chairs scraped as I passed. People quickly glanced over their laptops, and the girl behind the counter paused mid-pour.

I didn't stop.

Couldn't.

He noticed me about halfway through.

I saw his posture shift, his head tilt slightly, and curiosity flicker across his features.

A small crease formed between his brows. Interest, maybe?

Confusion?

He was watching now.

Just me.

My fingers fumbled in my bag as if they had a mind of their own, digging for a business card. My business card. A part of me wondered if this was completely insane. I was about to give a total stranger my info, like it was just business.

Trying desperately to trust my damn instincts.

My last steps landed me in front of him. Seeing him lock onto me completely. His golden eyes narrowed just enough to make room for intrigue.

Those eyes were seeing my vulnerability, undressing my insecurities, and caressing me where I stood.

Just when I thought I had made a tragic mistake… he smiled.

I could feel every eye on me. But I didn't care. With a shaken grip, I scribbled my personal number on the reverse side of the card, then my hand reached for his. It was warm. Grounded. I placed the card gently in his palm. His gaze dropped to it, then back up to me. I saw the moment he read 'salon' and something sparked. Like he hadn't expected that. Like he liked it.

I felt fire rise inside me. My heart was beating to an ancient rhythm.

My anxiety, running rampant as my mind strayed to moments when I was comfortable in his embrace. I could feel the animalistic choreography as he moved inside me. His presence evoked a visceral longing for something ... primal, permanent, penetrating. I was drowning... in him.

"Thank you," he said while looking directly into my soul.

He carefully placed the card in his pocket.

"Come see me." I said without breaking eye contact. He bit his bottom lip. I turned and walked away.

Each step towards the door felt harder than the ones coming over. My knees were weak. Blood buzzed in my ears. The whole cafe felt like it had tilted slightly off center. The jazz hadn't stopped, but it was background now, like a film score to whatever this was.

This was the moment of truth. If I turned back around and he was still looking, then I had him, and I had to have him. Slowly, I looked over my left shoulder and saw that he was still gazing in my direction.

Yup, he was all mine.

*****

Even with my sudden onset of exhaustion, I was on cloud nine, strolling through the faint breeze, allowing the sun to flirt with my skin. Though it didn't take long for a car to zip past, music blaring, and rancid smoke successfully escaping through its windows before it vanished west in the distance, but not before completely killing my vibe. That was the repulsive smell of Haze. This, however, should not be a surprise. It's 2070, and this is Nevermore, or rather, what it has become.

Nevermore, once a flourishing port town, historically vital for trade. Now desolate regions, where Devil's Haze devastated the population, surrounded these murky waters.

People label these areas Ash Zones, and only HellRat dealers visit them to profit from demise. Only haze-heads, caught in the drug's deadly grip, occupy Ash Zones. Identified by a deep gray ashen complexion, and vacant, deep-set, haunted, hollow eyes. These zones were their domain, but further north, in the skyline's pulse, where crumbling row-homes brush against neon luxury high-rises, something different rules the air.

Hover Lords, descendants of dirt bike crews, a tradition born before hover tech took over. Back when tires kissed pavement and wheelies sliced through traffic. Now, hover-bikes, patched together with military-grade scrapyard tech and swapped parts from classic automobiles no longer in production, zip through Far-side freely.

Dipping under officer drones and zooming by floating surveillance effortlessly. Flying in tight swarms like hornets. Labeled a menace by politicians, but the people understand that Hover Lords serve the community as protection. They frequent the places so close to the Ash Zones the city has disregarded. This is the place I was born, the city I love, and I'm determined to help build something here, to be proud of, again.

A steady stride led me to my destination, the historic arts & culture district of Mount Verne. Approaching a corner brick facade, wrapped in picture windows, framed in hand-carved art, with ivy creeping along its edges. Admiring a sidewalk garden, the length of the building and brimmed with a variety of herbs, vegetables, and flowering plants. I observed an Amethyst Sign glowing above the door boldly displaying "Beauty and the Beet"; this was my domain. A raw juice bar and a natural hair salon.

Two years ago, I opened my dream business.

My aunt Titi helped with every detail, from finding the location to decorating. The design framing the front windows was carved by her, and she made the salon mirror by hand, also inspiring the original idea and helping with the concept, as well as the menu. Beauty and the Beet was equally our creation. Aunt Titi said she wanted to make sure I had something of my own that I would be sure to protect.

Stepping inside, I saw my best friend, Skylar, was behind the bar. Her boyfriend, Mark, stood leaning on the other side, one arm resting on the surface as he watched Skylar move about.

I greeted them both. Mark looked up with a tender smile. "What's up, Yanni Giiiirl?" He drew out playfully before reaching out to give me a welcoming hug.

Mark Moore was a tall, slim, adorably soft-spoken, and overall personable guy. His curly tresses spilled over onto his forehead, the tips randomly streaked with a bright color blue. His smooth, light complexion had sprinkles of cinnamon.

The freckles that covered his nose, cheeks and framed his smiling, almond-shaped eyes, were notably a work of art.

He was wearing a baggy pair of paint-stained overalls, the uniform of a rather gifted visual artist.

Daily, he would drop off Skylar, watch her set up for work while she not so subtly ignored his presence.

After a while, Mark would leave for his studio, a little further north from here, where he would mastermind mixed media and digital masterpieces that sold for top dollar, time and time again.

Mark had all that a once-struggling artist could ever ask for, but to him none of that compared to his most cherished companion.

Skylar Brooks. A slim, nerdy, upbeat, beautiful wild child with short and curly bright pink tresses. Skylar was both a history buff and a computer genius. I have known Skylar since elementary school. We were more like sisters than friends from the start.

During middle school, Skylar's grandmother became ill, so my aunt took her in to live with us. Since then, we have spent every single year together, except for one. After graduating high school, Skylar journeyed to a prestigious technology institute. But before the year was out, Skylar was right back home. I never knew exactly what happened during the time she was away; I was just ecstatic to have her back.

Mostly, she works here with me, running the juice bar and styling hair part-time, while I focus on styling exclusively.

On Fridays, she DJs our weekly happy hours, when Titi comes in to man the bar. Together, we all form the perfect team.

Our menu hosts a few of my family's recipes, passed down by my Aunt Titi herself. Some have been my favorites since before I can even remember. Like the "Sun Kissed Refresher", made with pineapple, mango, orange, coconut water, and lime zest. Titi used to say, "Don't feel down, baby, here's a cup of sunshine." She made me this every time I was sad, and my troubles melted away. Another favorite of mine I call "The Honey Hex". It's made with apple, golden pear, raw local honey, chamomile, and vanilla bean. Titi gave me this after my very first heartbreak, and it dried away my tears.

"Sky-Sky!" I greeted as I stepped behind the counter.

"My-Ya!" she replied without pausing for a moment.

Sky was stocking the shelves with produce and jamming to Afro Beats blaring from the front speaker while simultaneously listening to something in the bright neon-green earphones she wore daily.

Despite it being a little after 8:00 AM, Sky had almost finished stocking, and she had already watered the plants and wiped down the display window.

I plucked the right side of Skylar's earphone playfully while bumping my hip into hers. "Damn, girl, are you on speed? You're just in this bitch on autopilot!" I said as the music paused.

In one motion, Mark had reached over the bar, grabbing the remote and stopping the music. A news report had caught his eye. He unmuted the TV mounted on the wall above the mirror behind the bar.

"See you girls playing around while real shit out here going on!" Mark stated as he adjusted the volume so we all could hear the news report.

Our attention went to the screen.

A depressing scene.

Footage of protestors pumping signs in the air that displayed colorful phrases like "We're gonna claw back", "Justice for NO-more!", "Crabs get cracked" and my favorite, "Dew right by the bay!"

The footage then cut to vivid images of what they were protesting.

The video displayed officers in their uniformed wetsuits, officially titled "Bay Patrol," lurking along Nevermore's famous Inner Harbor, like killer sharks. Videos flashed across the screen as they beat up helpless fishermen, invaded and destroyed their boats in the search for contraband.

"Fucking crabbers!" Mark spat, his tone saturated with disgust. "Like none of this shit is actually called for, for real." Crabbers had become the people's nickname for the bay patrol, who offered rewards for the reporting or "clawing" of crab runners.

"Fucking crabbers…" Skylar agreed, her tone bleak. "It makes you wonder, though. Is this what they expected to happen when they enacted the Crustacean Protection Act in 2043? I mean, are they really protecting the Bay? Or was the Environmental Protection Agency formed to terrorize people who look like us under the guise of enforcing the ban on crabs?"

Mark's face twisted in genuine disgust. "Who is part of clawback culture other than people like us? And that ain't limited to fucking skin complexion, Sky. It's a matter of class." Mark hoisted himself onto the barstool and continued. "That's why they started calling this city NO-More! Nevermore was synonymous with the Chesapeake Blue Crab. And it transformed from a regional delicacy to a black market treasure almost overnight."

Skylar moved closer to the bar now, her attention on us both. "Everything I know about crabs I've learned either from Titi's recollection or in history books. But I gotta be honest with you, I always called bullshit. Severe ecological collapse, over-harvesting, and a widespread mutation caused by increased pollution apparently led Nevermore to declare crabs protected. To me, it aways sounded…no pun intended," she paused, "fishy." She said with a shrug.

"Yeah, and the damn Crab Act made it illegal to trap, cook, sell, or even possess Chesapeake crabs." Mark continued, "To us, the crab was way more than food though. For people like my Daddy's Daddy, it was history. For families who found their livelihood in crab culture, it was identity. Shit, my Pops says these waters are not the same anymore. To Nevermore, the crab ban threatened way more than a culinary sensation. The ban destroyed our culture. Motherfuck these crabbers, man." Mark muted the TV and slammed down the remote.

Mark was not only a successful artist, but he was also a hardcore graffiti activist. He secretly displayed his work as murals throughout the city and throughout the areas they called "Tha' Barrows," where sometimes people sold crabs illegally.

His most memorable pieces depicted agents as crabs in uniform, being attacked with giant mallets, tagged with messages like, "The only good crab is the one we eat." That's how he got his start as an artist.

There was no doubt in my mind that this had sparked new inspiration for Mark today. Skylar would not likely see him until sometime tomorrow, as he took his frustration out on abandoned buildings instead of canvas.

"Alright, my fly girl," Mark addressed Skylar, walking over to her and placing the sweetest kiss upon her brow. "I'm off to change the world, one paintbrush stroke at a time," he chuckled, grabbing his bags and heading for the door. Skylar rolled her eyes toward the sky.

"Mark, please be safe out there today." I pled.

He turned towards me and motioned with a raised fist. "To Nevermore!"

And with that, he vanished through the door.

"That boy will get his ass arrested one day," I added with a sigh.

Skylar exhaled slowly. "And that's his ministry, girlie, not ours." She shrugged again. "All that money he makes, and he's still determined to cause trouble to make a statement." She shook her head with vigor as if she were resetting her train of thought.

"Your first appointment is at 9 o'clock, right?" She asked, "You already know I made you a fresh green juice. It's on your station next door," she said, not missing a beat. This juice, which is called "The Green Spark," made with kale, green apple, cucumber, celery, kiwi, lime, and spirulina. This was my Titi's remedy for exhaustion. These got me through college exams, late-night study sessions, and early morning classes.

I smiled and blew her a kiss; she took a moment to catch it in the air, then went right back to work. I pushed through the French doors to enter the salon.

The familiar scent of fresh lavender greeted me at the door. I took a deep breath, savoring the calm before the storm. At my station, the green juice was waiting for me, just as Sky promised. As I prepped my tools, I couldn't help but replay the encounter with the mysterious man from the cafe over and over in my mind. His golden eyes, his magnetic presence, it was like something out of a dream. I melted all over again. Shaking my head, I tried to regain my focus. Today was a busy day, and I needed to keep my mind on my clients.

Just as I finished setting up, my first client of the day, Mrs. Jenkins, walked in. She was a regular, always coming in for her weekly wash and steam treatment. Mrs. Jenkins did not need to come in every week, but she said the salon felt like a safe space, so for two years, she's seen me weekly, and her presence was comforting. Something familiar. She shared stories of her youth, told me about a time Nevermore was a place of shining stars, and urged me to be careful in what our world has become. Mrs. Jenkins offered the sweetest embrace before she left, thanking me for her appointment and reminding me she would see me at the same time next week, as always.

My day ran smoothly, with each client in my chair filling a different space. As much as I was servicing them, they all did something for me, each filling in a unique piece to the puzzle. I worked diligently until I finally had a moment to breathe. I went next door to find Sky wiping down the counter, jamming to something playing in her ears. When she saw me, she took off her headphones and smiled. "Hey punk," she said with a bright smile.

"Sky-Sky," I took a seat at the counter. She scurried to grab something from the fridge, then returned, placing a freshly made acai bowl in front of me. I swear this was a work of art. Hues of berries, sliced bananas, coconut slivers, and golden granola sprinkles, topped with a drizzle of honey that glistened in the light like a thread of gold. All sketched across a canvas of smooth, cold purple bliss.

I took my first bite slowly, making sure I got everything: the acai, a slice of banana, a few berries, and just enough granola for the right amount of crunch. I let the cold hit my tongue before dropping my shoulders and relaxing into every bite.

"So, what do we have planned for the rest of the day?" she asked.

"Umm, work bitch, I'm doing it now," I replied. "It's a freaking Monday, for God's sake; at least let's get to midweek before you start that shit."

"AND?! Girl, the world's too big not to explore, party, bullshit, and fuck up in!"

"The beginning of the week," I reminded.

"Life is short; it could be the week's end."

"Morbid as hell!"

"Or", she interjected abruptly, "alive, as fuck."

"Life is not an amusement park, Sky." I skimmed the spoon like a brush across canvas.

"Your place is too big for a constant party of one."

"And you have a harem…in a studio apartment," I replied, shaking my head, but smiling at her carefree consciousness.

"Yes, I love my different flavors," she winked.

"And what about Mark?" I reminded. "You have a man, remember?"

"Girl, is *that* what you call him?" She chuckled, "Let loose, baby, it does wonders for the complexion!" Her tone more serious now, "Ethical non-monogamy, Yanni, it's really a thing. My *man* is cool, fool." I rolled my eyes, then paused, remembering this morning's encounter. Blood rushed to my cheeks. Her eyes narrowed, knowing. "Yanni, what's going on?"

"Nothing really." I paused again to reflect, his eyes cutting through my thought process. "I just kind of met someone this morning," I finally replied. Basking in the memory of him. "I swear to God, Sky, he was just…unreal." I exhaled and relaxed into the seat.

"Yanni!" she blurted, her surprise uncontainable. "Tell me more," she demanded with genuine joy.

"I met him at the cafe," I explained. "Sky, he had these… alluring eyes, and it was like they spoke directly to me."

"Damn, what did they say?" She asked with a hint of a smile, though she wasn't entirely kidding.

"More than what they said, they…" I stammered, "claimed.." I continued. Now, her gaze contained pride with an equal amount of concern. "But it's not that deep. No time for romance. I built all this myself. I'm not risking it for a fairytale."

"Yanni," her disappointment clear in her discourse, "if you dismiss him before you even invite him in… how will that kitty ever get pet?"

I reached for the dishrag on the counter, swinging it playfully in her direction. "My kitty gets pet just fine, ma'am!"

"Self touch does not fucking count," she managed to get out through her solo symphony of chuckles. "You're gonna get arthritis before you turn thirty, you keep that shit up!"

"Skylar, it's more to life than sex."

"Like what? Oral?"

"I swear you are the poster child for uncouth," I said, rolling my eyes.

"Brazen," she beamed. "But seriously, if sex only serves to make humans we never asked for, then why would our gracious creator give us so many incredible positions?"

"Some might argue the act *is* asking for the humans, Skylar."

"Like, 'The Folded Lotus.' You did that shit before?"

"You're ridiculous." I shook my head, holding back laughter.

"Reverse Cowgirl" bent over, shaking her bottom from side to side.

"Grow up!" I howled.

"The Jackhammer."

"Now you're pushing it," I warned

"The Wheelbarrow!"

"What the fuck is wrong with you?" I laughed almost uncontrollably.

"The Rocking Horse!"

"Now I'm getting up," I threatened.

"The Don't Fall Off."

"Sky, give me a fucking break!" I said, falling back in my chair.

"The Lazy Susan."

"Graceless..."

"The Butter Churner."

"Gutter Snipe!" clutching my imaginary pearls.

"The Standing Ovation."

"Sky, bite me!" I had had more than enough.

"Ayana," she playfully flicked her tongue, "tempt me."

"Lawd, what in the name of sin did I just walk into?" Titi's voice sliced through, her wide hips swaying to the beat of her footsteps. She carried a small bouquet of fresh lavender, tied in tan twine, an offering of peace... or a warning.

"You running a salon or a whorehouse, chérie?" She said, unhooking the brittle stems from the door. She replaced them with a fresh bundle like a sacred ritual. "Lord Sky, you're supposed to be helping her, not corrupting the child! Can't a woman come see her babies without hearing about butter churning and back shots before noon?" She teased, "I haven't even had my damn tea yet," a subtle demand.

Sky moved to prepare a cup of tea for my auntie as I grabbed her bag and placed it in the back for safekeeping.

"Titi, come hell or high water, you bring that lavender up in here every single week," Skylar grinned, handing her a fresh cup of tea.

"And will," Titi replied, adjusting her bangles with a smirk before taking a sip. "Keeps the devil out and keeps you in check." She teased. "I tell y'all time and time again this city is full of forces that mean ya no damn good. I carved protection right on the surface of the building with my own bare hands to keep it out of here."

"Titi, not with the evil talk, please," I pleaded.

"Then don't get me started! Anyway, are you ladies coming by the Griot's Groove later this week? I could use some help setting up. Plus, some fancy DJ is replacing the band this week, and I'm sure a certain busybody, bright-haired Wildchild would enjoy him." She said, now speaking to Skylar.

My aunt was referring to a biweekly outdoor festival that ran from early spring to summer's end, the "Griots' Groove." It took place outside the Wheatley Museum, on Holiday Way. The Griots' Groove was home to local vendors carrying everything from art and vintage books to neo-knick-knacks, vinyl records, and down-home cuisine. Titi had a booth where she sold living plants, dried herbs, and eclectic jewelry.

"Titi, you already know, we are there," Skylar exclaimed, for both of us

I looked up, and my aunt was staring at me with an inquisitive look.

"What?" I asked through a frown.

She grimaced. "Now I know you lyin', 'cause when we forget to mind our tone, huh?"

"I'm sorry," I apologized, honestly meaning no harm. "I just wanted to know why you were staring a hole into my soul."

She didn't answer right away, just eyed me like she was about to turn a page. Then she leaned back and flashed that half smile I'd known my whole life. "Nothing," she said, too smooth to mean it genuinely. "You just got a little shine on ya, that's all."

Skylar whipped her head around and, in a hushed tone, asked, "Wait, did something happen?"

"No," I said a little too fast, causing her to raise a questioning brow.

"Y'all are reading too much into my face when it's resting," she grinned. "And you're right, you grown, but I know when my baby got her mind stuck on something. And you look exhausted." Titi and Sky locked eyes.

"It's nothing," I added before a sudden movement caught my eye. Jerking my head in its direction, I could have sworn the mirror's reflection behind the juice bar folded. And before I had time to refocus and shake it off, I could have sworn I heard a faint whisper, "The Last Broussard."

Now that I had shaken it off and was looking up again, I witnessed Sky and Titi share a strange look before Titi rested her attention back on me. No words, just a stern stare.

We shared a few laughs over tea before Titi bid us adieu, threatening loss of life if she did not see us this week at the festival. Thankfully, the rest of the day flew by, and before I knew it, Sky and I were tidying up, gathering our belongings, and walking out the door.

2

SMOKE & MIRRORS

(Eli)

Frozen, I watched her as she walked away. Unsettled, part of her was pulling me. I wanted to follow. Needed to.

It was something about her. That fearless energy.

Her eyes.

Her eyes beckoned, like a dare.

Most people turned away when I stared. Like their spirits warned, an incomprehensible force played on their minds, leaving them with a sense of unnerving mystery.

Not her.

She didn't just hold my gaze; she lulled me in closer. Like she wanted me caught in her trap.

She left me there, the air thick around me.

Who the fuck was she?

The question followed me, even after I started my ignition and drove away.

The atmosphere, gray and eerie as I shifted through the streets of Nevermore like a shadow. Passing crumbling murals and rusted fences. Every mile away from that coffee shop felt like a mistake I couldn't undo.

The warehouse sat just outside the Ash Zone, surrounded by the ghosts of buildings long abandoned. No one comes around this part of

Nevermore. Well, not the smart ones, anyway.

I parked around back and entered through the rear steel doors.

Jay was waiting inside, mouth tense, like somebody stole his fucking bike.

"Y-Y-You're late," Jay said, trying to sound like he ran the place. The stutter from childhood still clung to him, even when his jaw said otherwise.

"Do I clock in somewhere, motherfucker?" I brushed past him.

Jay wasn't just my right hand. He was my brother in everything but blood. In some ways, he understood me better than my real one. With every step I took toward power, he matched it.

I stepped further inside. The damp, musty air was almost overpowering.

Crates lined the walls, marked in symbols that only two people could read. Some held treasures we hadn't catalogued; others held things that... breathed.

"We've got a problem."

I didn't stop walking. "We always got problems."

"This one bleeds." I stopped.

The silence, heavy between us, was louder than anything he could've said.

"And who caused this...problem, Jason?"

Something ancient pressed behind my eyes. Not fire, older than flame. Alive. Watching. A beast licking its teeth behind glass.

It moved like it had its own will. Right now, it was promising to ignite.

For years, I didn't quite know what it was, only that it called out when I got too close to the edge.

"It was an honest mistake," he said softly

I turned to face him fully.

He didn't flinch, but his jaw tightened, like he knew I was deciding what kind of punishment could correct an "honest mistake."

The silence stretched long between us, and I let him sit right there in it.

The heat seeping through my skin wasn't mine. It crackled under the surface, prickling like a brand pressed too close but never touching. My fingers grazed the necklace through my shirt; the beast inside me was stirring.

I closed my eyes.

Not now. Settle down.

I exhaled slowly and steadily to find my calm, for now. "Show me."

I followed Jay past rows of stacked crates, through the dimly lit hallway in silence, the air heavy around us.

Where my footsteps felt disrupted, we stopped. Something warped and twisted the lock, as if melting it from the inside out, causing the steel door to hang on its hinges. Someone smeared across the concrete walls sigils that were once neatly placed.

The room, empty, a blanket, damp and wrinkled, abandoned in the corner.

My eyes ablaze, chest heaving as I placed my hand on the charm where it hung.

Jay spoke carefully. "She's gone."

"She?" I questioned.

"O–One of the n–new girls. N–No one s–saw her leave."

"And, Roderick," I asked, "where was he?"

"She had to h-ha-have to slipped right past him." He explained, "A mistake."

"We can't afford mistakes," I growled.

"She was here one minute and then the next she was gone." Jay whispered slowly.

I froze. Something felt off.

A glimmer caught my eye. Glass. Shattered.

Magical.

Not just broken. Violated.

My chest tightened.

No. No, no, no.

I took off down the hall. My boots echoed against the concrete, each step pulling me closer to what I didn't want to see.

The crate.

Open.

Empty.

The Mirror of Makaya was gone.

"Oh, he's dead," I hissed.

Storming through the damp halls and up the stairs to the office, I found Roderick.

He stood.

Then, he stumbled back, the concrete wall stopping him cold.

The surrounding air thickened.

Jay moved as if he knew what was coming, arm raised out of habit.

I let the flicker behind my eyes burn.

Heat crawled up my spine. I could taste Roderick's fear blooming in his sweat.

But something pulled me back.

Her eyes.

That look.

Like she dared me to follow.

Roderick slid down the wall, gasping as if he had barely escaped drowning.

He trembled.

My surrender had nothing to do with Jay

It was her.

The memory of her skin, her smoldering gaze, the way her presence claimed space like it belonged to her... it burned through me like wildfire.

"Jay, get a shipping container at the abandoned docks. We'll move the rest of the girls there."

I glanced at Roderick.

"Take him with you."

Then back to Jay. "But after today, he's my driver. Nothing more."

******

My pulse still outpaced my thoughts by the time I got home. I needed to be surrounded by silence, control…order.

People looked at the Regal Regency complex on Light Street and saw just another slice of gentrified Nevermore. The chromed brick facade, frosted glass entry, and polished steel balconies showed them nothing more than your typical luxury apartments. Only a few people who knew I owned the building knew the secrets held below.

I walked to the front door and scanned my key card to enter, walking into the low-lit lobby surrounded in matte black stone with copper accents. The polished marble floors echoed my steps. Passing the main elevators, I reached the bronze double doors and placed my palm on the keypad to reveal a private elevator. This led to a destination not displayed on any blueprint.

The underground level sat 50 feet below the surface, divided into three wings: living, leisure, and control.

The elevator opened onto a wide hallway that led directly to the formal living room. A long, low fireplace stretched across one wall; flames flickered behind tinted glass. Thick black columns held up the high arched ceilings. A false skylight overhead shifted with the time and weather above ground, casting a believable glow.

To the left, through a tall bronze archway, was the dining room. A smoky glass chandelier hung above the table. Past that, the kitchen sat clean and quiet. Black matte appliances, marble counters, no clutter in sight.

The right wing belonged to control. My study sat behind a seamless matte-black glass door. Beyond it was the climate-controlled vault that held my collection, art, relics, and a few things better left alone.

Past the study, the hallway led to the poolroom. Black tiles with golden grout lined the pool, and lights illuminated it from beneath. The water was calm. Still. Heated and waiting.

My living quarters were at the end of it all.

Nine hundred square feet of stillness. Black walls and ceilings. Gold trim. Amber lighting softened the hard edges. The mirrors had gold frames. An Alaskan King bed, low and wide, framed in black leather. A private spa, my bathroom, sat just beyond it, carved in smooth stone.

I was standing dead center in the paradise my sweat and blood created, thinking of her. She was chaos in silk, something primal

24

dressed as poetry. I should have run. I wouldn't.

This was my kingdom, carved from secrets. She was the only sound that cut through all this silence.

*****

I took a moment to get comfortable, then I sprawled across the plush sofa. The leather, cool against my skin. Low amber lights cast soft shadows across the room.

I was reaching for the remote when the ding of my private elevator interrupted me. I didn't flinch. "Right on time."

I stood, wrapping my mirror image in a familiar embrace. "Baby bro."

When I let him go, we bumped fists, locked thumbs, and flapped. Our hands became birds, just like when we were kids.

"Baby brother by forty seconds," he laughed

I laughed. "Hey, but who's keeping count, hmm?"

He grinned while scanning the space like he hadn't been here a dozen times before. "You know I love this crypt of yours." He paused. "Mysterious," he said in a goofy tone. "Are there vacancies in the building by any chance?"

"Ya know, I'm thinking about evicting the tenant in the penthouse!" I teased, "This fucker never pays the rent. "

He handed me a sleek bottle. "But he comes bearing a Macallan 18 Year Sherry Oak Single Malt Scotch."

I raised an eyebrow, taking the bottle like it was holy. "Well, damn. He might've just bought himself the summer." We laughed.

I was happy to see him. Sure, he lived just upstairs. But sometimes, we felt worlds apart.

We settled into the sunken lounge, the bottle between us, its amber glint catching the light.

Across from me, my twin. His gray eyes are a cool contrast to my hazel brown. Same jawline, carved by blood and fire, but a light in him I could never quite carry.

He poured for both of us. No words, just the quiet clink of glass and the comfort of being understood without explanation. I'd always been his shield. Through fire, through grief, and through things we still didn't have names for. That role never left me, even now, seated in comfort beneath layers of stone and wealth.

"Soooo," he sang in that deliberately annoying tone, drawing it out just to get under my skin, "how's the evil crime empire and all?"

He smirked over the rim of his glass like he hadn't just dropped a loaded joke in the middle of my peace.

"Empire?" I clutched my imaginary pearls. "Nah, just a little hobby. Maybe I'll begin charging admission. Front-row seats to the chaos."

We burst into uncontrollable laughter.

"Seriously, less handsome me," he said, topping off both our glasses. "You can always just come walk into the light."

I traced the rim of my glass for a moment, thinking.

"Thing is… we were born in the smoke, what good is it light there?" I took a sip. "I just learned how to breathe in this shit. "

He nodded slowly, eyes on the liquid fire in his glass.

"Yeah," he said, quieter this time. "But sometimes I wonder if you remember how to come up for air."

The silence after that wasn't heavy. Just honest.

He sipped, then leaned back further, letting the scotch roll across his tongue before speaking.

"Every relic I've come across? Something ugly always comes with it. Or a price too big to pay. Think they're holding history, but really, it's holding them."

He shook his head slowly. "It's never just the magic that's dangerous. It's what people turn into chasing it."

"That's when it becomes a weapon," I said. "But not all magic is blood and debt

Ali arched a brow. "Yeah? Then why don't you keep any for yourself if I'm so off base?"

"What if I told you I do?"

Ali leaned back, eyes narrowing just a little. "Then I'd say. Show me."

I let the silence stretch, then stood. "Come on."

In silence, we moved through the golden archway, the hush heavy with anticipation. The cool air of the relic room met us like a held breath. Ali's steps slowed; his usual jokes, forgotten for now.

His eyes scanned the room, soaking it all in. His gaze paused on a few objects, quiet but alert.

He pointed toward a narrow, weathered statue wrapped in copper wire.

"That one's from the Kongo," I said. "It's called an Nkondi. Used to hunt down liars and thieves—people would drive nails into it to wake the spirit inside."

His eyes shifted to a wide, bowl-like disc etched in gold.

"That's an abamfa, of Ashanti origin. Ceremonial. They'd fill it with water or oil for ancestral blessings."

He tilted his head at a long knife displayed on black velvet.

"Tuareg blade," I added. "Northern Mali. Forged under moonlight, blessed with desert herbs. Never dulls."

Then his gaze dropped to a cracked black stone resting in a shallow dish.

"That's tepoztli, volcanic glass from the old Mexica lands. Used in rites... mostly the kind folks don't talk about."

I cut a sideways glance at him. "Don't pick that one up."

His attention, now on me. He was eyeing my necklace. "I guess some of this stuff is just impossible to let go."

"Yeah," I looked away now.

Ali's eyes were still roaming when I crossed the room and uncovered the pedestal in the far corner.

"This one," I said.

The drum stood alone. A djembe, all white, smooth and pale like bone washed in moonlight. The ropework was gold, tight, and clean. No carvings, just silence pressed into wood.

Ali blinked. "That's real?"

"Very," I said, running a hand along the edge. "It's called Nsuma Nhyira. Spirit's Blessing."

He stepped in, curiosity piqued. "Where's it from?"

"Ghana. Legend says it carries the heartbeat of ancestors who healed their people with sound. When you play it right, it can soothe pain, calm restless spirits, even mend the broken."

Ali whistled low. "You ever play it?"

I shook my head. "It's not waiting for a player. It's waiting for a purpose."

Ali gave a soft nod, eyes still lingering on the drum for a moment before he stepped back.

"Well," he said quietly, "that's... something."

The energy shifted, gentle now.

I let the silence breathe before speaking. "Come on. Let's eat."

He gave a faint smile. "Yeah. That sounds good."

3

ASHES IN THE WIND

(Yah-Yah)

Today started just like any other. The sweet sound of neo-soul surged through the shop as the soothing smell of orange blossom and fresh eucalyptus warmed the air.

I moved through the shop on autopilot, preparing my space. I set out all the proper tools of the trade and finished preparing a growth-stimulating oil for a client.

My products, crafted by my own hands, are unique. No science, no ratio, no formulas, just pure instinct.

My hands always seemed to know what people needed before they said a word.

By the time my first client slid into the chair, I'd already steeped a tea to lift her spirits before even knowing she was grieving. I didn't question it. I never do.

But lately, that quiet tug in my gut has felt heavier, like something just beneath the surface is shifting.

She said little when she came in. She just gave me a soft smile before settling into the chair like her bones were tired. Some clients need conversation. Others just need to be held together for a while. A moment to loosen their own grip on things, allowing them to relax while I become that glue, it's our bond.

"Long week?" I asked gently, the cape's scent of lavender filling the air as I draped it around her.

"Well, that's one way to put it," she wearily replied.

Her energy was frayed. Grief. Fresh.

"I made you something, Mama," I breathed. "Tea, chamomile, passionflower, and just a pinch of ashwagandha."

She paused briefly, then whispered, "You always seem to know."

After her shampoo, I moved through her coils slowly, my fingers coated in the oil I made before she arrived.

My client let out a long breath as I worked; the kind that came from somewhere deeper than stress.

At first, she sat in silence.

I didn't push. I just let the rhythm of twisting do the soothing.

Her energy, heavy, like she had been carrying around a storm that now, just a little, was becoming clear.

By the time she left, her shoulders were sitting a little lower, her breath calmer.

That's the goal. To help my tribe feel lighter.

As my client left the shop, the lights dimmed and flickered subtly. A power surge followed by the acrid smell of burning wires. This happened often. Like something was sucking up all the power and leaving very little for my space to use.

And every once in a while I would hear strange sounds from below the shop, sounds I couldn't explain.

I was wiping my station when I heard the familiar click of the front door.

When she stepped inside she was brushing an unknown substance off her shirt at the doorway. No telling where she'd been.

My Titi moved like she belonged in every room, and her hips coulda had their own soundtrack.

I stepped into her hug without hesitation, breathing in clove and camphor. She leaned back just enough to look into my eyes. "Now you know I done told you, you gotta burn sage up in here before you start your day, baby."

I rolled my eyes. "Now, how do you know I didn't"? I asked with a smile.

"And now I guess I got fool plastered right on my forehead dead and center."

Her eyes swept the room as if she could see things I couldn't. Maybe she could.

"And where is my Wildchild, Sky?" she asked, looking perplexed.

"She didn't come in today because she said she had Mark drama." I answered.

"Now, you and I both know that boy worships the ground she walks on; any drama she likely brought upon herself." She laughed, "probably walked it right in wrapped and dressed in a bow." She added.

Titi swayed her way to the bar, where she grabbed a cup like she owned the place.

I joined her, happy to be in her space

"You feel it, don't you?" she said, not looking at me.

I paused before sitting. "Feel what?" I questioned.

"That itch. The pressure building. Dreams you don't remember, but you wake up sweating, anyway."

My hand froze.

Now, facing me, sipping slowly. "You feel it." She questioned.

I shrugged, laughed, "Maybe I'm just tired. Work's been heavy."

She didn't smile. I leaned against the counter, folding my arms.

She took another sip, then set the mug down slowly and gently, as if she were placing it on holy ground. "Well, I don't know what it is, but I'm telling you now, baby, this ain't the time to be caught slipping." She placed her hand on mine. "Trust your gut," she continued

Her words.

Heavy.

"I don't know."

"You ain't gotta know. Just listen."

She pulled me into another hug, then pinched me as she gritted through closed teeth. "And burn the goddamn sage." She said before her exit.

Now the shop was nice and settled into its usual rhythm, but something still felt off.

A nagging unease that couldn't let up. Like a shadow brushing against me, trying to jog my memory.

When the bell over the door jingled, I looked up, expecting to see a familiar face, but I had never seen the woman who stepped inside. Her smile, polite, but it didn't reach her eyes.

As she stepped closer, a familiar chill slid down my spine.

I couldn't say why, but her presence felt like a crack in the calm.

I gently greeted her with a "Hey," my voice full of warmth. "Are you looking for something?"

She glanced at the fridge, then pointed. "A drink?"

I nodded and walked over. "What kind of day are you having?"

She didn't answer immediately. "One I want to forget."

I reached for a blend I'd bottled this morning. "Try this one. Good for settling nerves."

She took it with both hands, sipped, and then exhaled like she'd been holding her breath.

"You alright?" I asked.

She gave a tiny nod, eyes still scanning the space. "Yeah. Just… this place feels safe."

I didn't know what to say about that, so I stayed quiet.

She reached to pull out money to pay, but I stopped her. "On the house," I smiled

She smiled, "thankyou."

I watched until the door closed behind her.

When I was safe and alone inside, I locked it.

Yeah, I think it's quitting time.

I flipped the sign on the door to closed.

Home was calling.

Then I saw it.

On the ground in front of the shop was the strange mirror I had imagined in a daydream.

It was now right in front of me.

"The fuck?" I gasped.

4

BURNING QUESTIONS

(Eli)

My fists propelled forward, hitting the heavy bag with a tight rhythm. My body coiled, moving with precision. The swing of the bag made the chains rattle above me. Each dull thump traveled through my bones, but I continued with perfect form until my shoulders burned, my forearms were shaking, and my back was slick with sweat.

I came here to get empty.

She was still inside my head.

Stuck in the moment I last saw her, her hips stiff, frozen, mute, as I stupidly let her walk away without barely saying a word. Now I was alone in the gym, trapped in the ache she left behind, chest heaving, and heart pounding like it was trying to break free.

I tore off the gloves, exposing raw hands. My knuckles tingled, my chest tight with everything I was holding inside.

I headed to the back, towel clutched at my waist like a last defense.

I pressed my palm against the sauna door.

The steam curled around my skin, slow and persistent, like it had been waiting just for me. The terry cloth clung as I tried to sit still, but she was everywhere. Her eyes held me, like a dare, as I chased them without intention.

I was wondering how she'd taste when the thought pulled, pushed, then pulsed, thick and unforgiving. I shifted; this pressure, too sharp to be fantasy. It was a slow possession, dragging me under with each breath.

I trembled, jaw clenched, heart hammering, giving in to the weight of her.

Leaning forward, elbows on my knees, I let the silence settle.

Then, I remembered the business card.

I have to see her…in person.

******

Like a coiled predator, I waited, still, but not at rest. Breathing slowly, shallow, measured, and patient. Her scent hung so thick in the air, I could taste her. Heat was crawling up my neck and running down my back like I stepped too close to a fire; I shouldn't touch. I stood there, listening, watching.

I had to have more.

Not a want, but a need. The kind that exists beyond the body and lives in the blood. It's more than lust. It's internal gravity.

Each breath feeds its desire.

My hunger shifts, tightening the coil.

I watch, wait.

Her laughter echoed from behind the glass.

I stepped closer to the window and let my fingers trace the frame. A subtle warmth spread through my fingers, and the surrounding air shifted.

Something was pushing me back.

Easy. Not loud. Just a whisper against my skin, like a door clicking shut in the dark.

My stomach, uneasy.

No.

No, it couldn't be.

Something about the texture of the weathered, deep, and dark wood felt wrong.

At first glance, it looks decorative. Then the symbols appeared, tucked within the grooves. Dark circles, crossed by lines, strange shapes floating in space, with various dots arranged like stars.

They move.

The prickle under my skin flared.

The power wasn't obvious, but it was right there, carved directly into the wood.

None of this is decoration.

This is a ward!

This was magic carved and hidden with purpose. Whoever did this hadn't done it for show. They were protecting her. But from what, though? From who?

I pulled out her card, staring at her full name, Ayana Broussard-Carrol.

Broussard.

Something about that name.

If I couldn't go inside, I would wait until she came to me.

When the doors opened, she stepped out, trapped in my gaze and I in hers. Until.

"Yanni?" Her friend spoke in a questionable tone, breaking us out of a trance.

"Sky," Ayana stammered, "I'm sorry, this is…"

"Eli." I extended my hand to the slim, bright pink-haired, curious friend. "And you are?" I asked.

"This is Skylar, my best friend." Ayana blurted as her friend smiled, returning my embrace.

"I see I didn't catch you before quitting time." I directed my attention to Ayana. Oblivious to the warning blaring behind her. I saw now that whoever placed the protective layer here had done it privately. She had no clue what it was, or that it was even there.

"Because we met before 8 am, and now's when you decide to take me up on my offer?" She scoffed, her look stern, piercing. Daring. "Boy bye, I've got shit to do." She turned to lock her door.

"Okay," her friend added with concern, "standing out here, giving very much stalker where the fuck is my man to make sure we're safe out here?"

I laughed, "I just…wanted to see you again." Really, E? That's the best you can do? I wanted to turn and run in the opposite direction. "Well, I know you're headed out, but I'd like to take you out when you find the time."

She smiled.

I melted, more.

"Okay, well, let's start like normal people." The corners of her lips curl.

"Right!" the friend again. "Out here looking like you're trapped in a Shakespearean psychological thriller," both comedic and yet defensive, "would it have pained you to bring this girl a flower or something?"

So, a tag team? Oh, E, they're on your ass good. "Okay," I laugh, "my bad."

"Sky chill," now that look again, pulling me closer, "Why don't you call me? Tonight?"

"Tonight," I nodded.

Then once again, I was standing there as she walked away.

And this time, I knew exactly what I was losing if I didn't call.

5

DANCING WITH FIRE

(Yah-Yah)

"Straighten it out, baby," Titi called out to me from across the lot. "We *stay* put together."

I shook my head but straightened the banner on her booth, anyway. I didn't even have to turn around to know she was giving me her signature side-eye.

Skylar snickered, not helping.

"Y'all really gotta chill," I muttered, stepping back to check the alignment, even though we all knew it'd been straight enough five minutes ago.

Skylar lay back in her signature headphones, seated in a metal folding chair and puffing on a vape, replied, "Oh, I'm chill." She was carefree and pretty much worthless to me concurrently.

I understood somewhat. Mark had just left the booth after blatantly displaying his disgust for something they had been arguing about on their way to the festival. It was pretty clear Skylar was slowly drifting away from him, whether she wanted to or not.

Titi's booth was like the love child of a health food store and a conjure shop. Bundles of dried herbs hung from the corners, and glass jars and handmade candles lined the table, some filled with oils, others with stones. A carved wooden sign above it read *2thaRoot*.

I was putting out the last of Titi's inventory when I saw him.

Carrying a black duffle bag, his fresh white sneakers forged forward with a certain urgency.

Black ripped slim-fit jeans belted at his waist. A black graphic tee hugged his muscular frame, and a gold chain gleamed over the collar. His locs dropped wild and golden at his shoulders, catching the light as he moved.

We locked eyes for a moment. Just long enough to make me wonder if he was walking toward me. But before I could even blink, someone else ran up from the opposite direction.

He dropped the duffel at his feet and pulled the other man into a hard embrace. A movement muscle-deep and familiar. When they stepped apart, their hands kept moving in sync: fists connecting, thumbs interlocking, wings fluttering between them.

And that's when I saw the other man's face.

His brother.

A mirror image, same height, same frame, same locs. But his eyes… pale, smoky gray.

Twins.

Skylar, who had clearly remembered my full description of Eli, turned to me, wide-eyed. "Wait, so it's two of them?"

"Now, how do you two know the DJ?" Titi chimed in from behind the table.

"Choooooooo, Choooo," Skylar said, dragging out the sound like a damn train whistle, with all the maturity of a middle schooler.

I rolled my eyes and looked back over just in time to see him pull an all-white djembe from the duffle and hand it to his twin.

His brother looked overjoyed, grinning so wide that it split across his face as if someone had just handed him a piece of his soul.

They embraced again, then Eli glanced over at me.

This time, he didn't look away.

He said something to his brother, then advanced with a steady stroll. Those eyes locked on me.

"Hey you," he said when he reached the booth, voice low and warm. "Didn't mean to distract your entire crew."

I lifted an eyebrow. "Beautiful Drum" was all I offered as a reply.

He smiled, then nodded toward his brother, who hovered just a few steps behind, drum in hand.

"This is Ali," he said.

"His much more attractive twin brother," Ali added, extending his hand.

I shook it, then introduced my aunt and Skylar.

"DJ Ali-One," Titi called out to Ali, "We spoke earlier, but who knew there were two of you?" She laughed while motioning for him to come closer.

The three of them exchanged friendly banter while Eli beckoned me with that penetrating stare. And for a moment, the world went mute.

I hadn't realized Titi had attempted to get my attention.

"Gal, if you don't come help your poor auntie finish," her demand disguised in a friendly tone.

"I gotta help my baby brother with sound check," Eli said, glancing toward Ali, "then if it's cool, I'll come find you."

"Sure," I said, smiling.

Back at the booth, Skylar was rifling through Titi's crates.

"Sky," Titi said, without even looking up, "get outta there before something bites your lil nosy ass."

"I was just looking, Auntie," she pouted, dragging out the last word for effect.

Titi turned her focus to me now. "And you, gonna stand there looking love-struck while auntie does everything?"

I blinked, caught mid-stare in the direction Eli had walked off.

"I'm helping," I mumbled.

"Mmm," she said, pulling a bundle of lemongrass from the crate. "Helping yourself to an eyeful of sin and lust while your auntie works like a field hand in this smoldering heat. Get over here before I charge you booth rent."

Skylar laughed. "That man said I'll come find you, and now she's floating somewhere over Nevermore."

I grabbed a stack of small bags and started arranging them on the table, doing my best to focus. But my smile gave me away.

Just as I was finishing up, a calm, clear voice, just loud enough to grab attention, spoke. She welcomed the crowd, shouted out the vendors, and encouraged everyone to enjoy themselves before we heard the name we were waiting for.

Dj Ali-One.

The beat crept through the speakers, deep. Deliberate. Sinking in just heavy enough to catch your chest and make you lean into it.

His hand gently graced the turntables as he ensured the next track would blend perfectly in time.

Layers of jazz wove through a faint percussion, and it felt like it was speaking directly to me.

I turned toward the small stage just in time to see Ali step forward, djembe strapped across his torso, mic pointed at the drum. No words, no talking to the crowd. Just the steady rhythm of his hands meeting skin.

The sound layered over the track as if someone had composed it inside the original. Clean. Alive. His drumming didn't follow the beat; it molded it. He pulled in each instrument to serve something deeper.

Everyone started drifting closer. Even the vendors looked up from their tables.

Skylar leaned to get a better view of the stage. "That's him?"

Titi nodded. "Sure…is."

I said nothing. I just watched.

The drum spoke louder than the music. Filling the air with something, like a memory.

A ritual.

He played as if he'd been born to do so. Like the drum was an extension of his will. And the crowd? The crowd moved with him.

"This child isn't just performing," Titi said, her eyes fixed on the stage. "This is ministry." She paused. "But it's something more than that drum."

Just as I wanted to brush her statement off as just another one of her cryptic displays, I saw something shift.

Looking around the crowd, I saw with new sight.

People who had carried invisible weight now moved like something had been lifted.

The grieving, the lonely, something inside them cracked open.

The hopeless, now filled with abundance.

And they rejoiced.

This wasn't just music.

This was healing.

Something sacred disguised as a beat.

Skylar appeared beside me, eyes wide and bright as she took it all in. She nudged me, grinning.

"Okay, I'm not even high, and I feel that shit. Come on, Ya, let's dance." Skylar's chipper request.

I laughed, full and from my gut. "Sky, you are high as a giraffe's ass!"

She shrugged like I wasn't wrong.

"Still, come on, girl, it's something about this beat!"

I was just happy to see her smiling.

It was like her heart was healing right in front of me.

The music moved us.

And we let it.

Somehow singing the answer in an ancient call and response, that we chanted in return until the rhythm slowed, easing into a softer, smoother tone.

I felt like I could cry. Like the rhythm had cracked something open in me, too.

The djembe slowed as he made his way back to the decks and began manipulating the music once more.

Then, I could feel him approaching.

Measured.

Magnetic.

I turned.

His eyes cascaded down a willing and waiting canvas.

He smiled. "I told you I would find you," spoken in a low tone that landed at my hips.

"Damn, I guess I ain't run far enough," I teased.

Without laughing, but holding my gaze he moved to close the space between us, "Wanna step away for a moment, to talk?"

I nodded.

******

We stepped into the museum, a house of marble, perfection carved into soaring arches and massive stone columns.

Our steps echo going further into the depths of silence. Just us two, surrounded by ancient masks and carved relics encased in glass on each side of us.

We moved slowly, past art pieces that watched with hollow eyes.

Painted wood. Weathered textures. Clay vessels etched with symbols that scream warnings.

I halted.

Briefly, I felt a whisper calling directly to me.

Terrified, I tried to ignore it. Not wanting to have to explain that at times my imagination leads before I can hold it at bay.

I turned toward the display on my right. A narrow figurine standing inside. Its face, smooth and eyeless. Mouth slightly open, like it had been captured in the middle of a chant. Gold flakes clung to the ridges of its base.

"What we see as art, someone else somewhere has to see it as memory." His voice, deep, velvet on the back of my neck.

I didn't turn right away. Instead, I stood still, pressing down the wave of attraction threatening to crawl out of my skin.

"Okay, philosopher," I said playfully, placing a hand gently on his chest.

He smiled. "I'm a collector," he said, eyes locked on mine. "So I know something beautiful when I see it."

I gave a small shrug, trying not to smile too hard, but betrayed by the warmth that was rising to my cheeks.

"Touche," I said, nudging his arm lightly.

He gazed.

That stare.

Like he was trying to learn me by heart.

Moving closer, in a hushed voice, he asked, "Truth only, if no one was looking, what in this building would you steal?"

I raised an eyebrow. "You're trying to get me arrested now?"

"Nah. I just wanna know what kind of trouble you'd pick."

I glanced as if I were actually considering it.

"There," I pointed to three black women on a massive panel, lounging like they owned the whole damn world. "Look at them. Unbothered, just draped in color and print and glitter like armor! I can see that on my wall in real life."

He leaned in, eyes following my finger. "Damn girl! You've got some expensive taste."

I shrugged, still looking at the painting.

"Not expensive. Sacred."

"Fair."

Stepping back just a little, he looked more serious now. "Thanks for saying yes, by the way. To this."

"I mean, you said you'd find me."

"And maybe I always will."

And with that, he turned and walked the other way, casually glancing at the art, flashing a glare.

I followed him down the hall as he slipped into a smaller space. No soaring ceilings. No crowd noise bleeding through. Just muted lights, dark wood floors, and shadows folding into corners.

He slowed as we passed a series of photographs, soft, bare shoulders, mouths parted. Each frame implied it had overheard something intimate.

He glanced back. "You like these?"

I nodded, stepping closer to one. A Black woman in profile, glowing in gold light, eyes closed like she were listening to her own heartbeat. The photo pulsed.

"I do," I managed to reply through a cracked whisper. "It's so… honest."

Closer now, I feel his heat on my arm.

"I like the way you look at things."

I turned.

Now I was standing in what he said. Feeling… observed. Maybe to him, I was art too.

Reaching out carefully, he pushed a loc behind my ear slowly. Watching me. Like he wanted to have his hands on me all day.

The space between us crumbled.

"This is starting to feel like a date, sir," I said, teasing but not moving away.

He touched my chin, gaze dropping to my lips. "It can be whatever you want it to be."

I didn't answer.

Not with words.

My hands moved curiously.

With the lightest touch.

Tracing along the line of his wrist

My fingers spelled out my desire until my hand cupped his jaw, my thumb grazing his bottom lip.

His breath deep and steady, patient. Leaning in. Slowly.

Giving me ample time to pull away.

I stay

His hands rested on the small of my back.

His lips meet mine with a question, asked slowly, softly, not a demand.

He kissed me like we had…all the time in the world, like his touch wanted to learn me.

Where could this lead?

How long could this last?

How does it taste?

I kissed him as if I knew all the answers.

Then, his forehead rested against mine, still close, breathing me in. His hand slipped from my back.

He stepped back.

"I think I like this," I told him.

His eyes never leaving mine as he said, "Then tell me when you fucking love, this shit."

I felt that. Deep.

Like he'd marked the moment without even touching me.

I didn't say anything right away. I just held his gaze, desperately trying to pretend I wasn't suddenly burning behind my ribs.

We moved further through the museum together.

We walked past abstract paintings and beautiful sculptures, strange shapes, and vivid colors. Our arms often brushed against one another, but neither of us pulled away.

We stopped.

This piece caught my eye.

Bright lines crossing over dark patches, like cracks in ancient wood.

It flickered, a quiet flame.

I catch him staring, his gaze different. Quiet. Like he was holding something back.

"Fire's not exactly my favorite memory," he said.

I took his hand.

"My mother died screaming in a fire I escaped." He paused. "Some sounds you never unhear."

I squeezed his hand, and my chest tightened.

"I know about pain that stays. My mother died on the same day as my father. Life's never been the same."

He nodded, eyes distant.

The silence spoke to both of our hearts.

Gently, I pulled my hand from his.

"We should probably get back outside," I said, already planning our escape.

He nodded, offering a weary smile.

"I think we could both use the fresh air."

Slowly, we walked to the exit, pushed the heavy glass doors, and escaped to the warm evening air.

Spoken-word flowed from the stage.

The sun dropped lower, casting a deep orange glow across the plaza

We walked through the crowd, still carrying something between us.

Glancing in his direction, I asked, "You good?"

His eyes lowered. "I think so. You?"

I squeezed his hand.

"Yeah...just...full."

"Yeah, same."

We didn't rush. We let the crowd move around us. The sweet sound of poetry folded into the background. Standing there in silence, the breeze brushes between us, lifting Egyptian Musk from his t-shirt. The scent was warm and familiar, like a scratchy jazz record or a warm embrace.

We stood in the silence, as if it belonged only to us. Then, a familiar squeal met us.

Skylar.

Her laughter cut through the crowd, light and shameless.

"Okay, look at y'all!" she said, strolling up with Ali at her side, both carrying something strong in red plastic cups. "Museum dates? Holding hands? We see that hot shit," she grinned, taking a sip.

A complete shift in the vibe. "Y'all are cute or whatever."

Ali raised his cup with a quiet smile, eyes flicking between the two of us. "I told her we should leave you two alone, but she doesn't listen."

"She never does," I said, side-eyeing Skylar.

Eli let out a low chuckle beside me, his hand still holding mine, fingers laced easily like they'd always been there.

Skylar nudged Ali. "Let's go get plates before the lines get crazy. Y'all coming?"

Eli glanced at me. I nodded.

"Yeah, we're coming," I said, not bothering to let go of his hand.

The evening was easy. Laughter, music, drinks, and conversations.

Eli stayed close, his arm often brushing against mine.

Skylar talked with her hands, expressing each word with just as much emotion as the last, while Ali held on to her every word with occasional outbursts of laughter.

At the night's end, the crowd had thinned, and the lights overhead buzzed a little louder against the quiet. We lingered at Titi's booth, clowning and helping her pack up.

Ali, eyes mostly on Skylar, said, "I need to get my gear from the stage and load up my truck, but when I'm done, y'all wanna go grab some drinks? I know a spot open late."

Skylar, without hesitation, nodded. "Say less."

I gave her a look but didn't argue. Then turned to Eli. "You driving?"

"Okay," he said, calm, unreadable.

The brothers made their way back to the stage, weaving through stacks of folding chairs and trash bins. From this distance, their gestures looked almost choreographed, until they didn't. Their gestures sharpened. Voices too low to hear, but their energy changed. Eli's hands moved more than usual. Ali stepped in closer.

It wasn't dramatic, but it *definitely* was a moment.

Skylar leaned toward me. "The fuck is wrong with them? They good?"

I didn't answer right away. Just watched Eli exhale slowly, then head for the truck.

"They will be," I said, more to myself than her.

I wasn't sure what I had just witnessed. Something in the way Eli had looked at his brother. Like he was biting back more than words.

Turning back to Titi's booth, I caught her concerned stare targeted directly at me...observing.

"You good?" she asked, casual on the surface, but her eyes said she didn't miss a thing.

"Yeah," I lied. Or maybe hoped. "Just...a long day."

She gave a slow nod.

"Mm. Well, y'all be safe out there. Act like you know and don't let my prayer be in vain."

"Always," I said, helping her shut the last crate.

Behind me, I heard the tailgate slam. Eli was ready.

******

Eli opened the passenger side of his convertible like a perfect gentleman. The soft leather hugged me as I settled in.

He eased into the driver's seat, with one hand on the wheel and the other resting on the gearshift. He glanced at me softly before starting the ignition. The engine purred as the city lights danced along the jet-black hood.

We passed through downtown's polished edges before the scenery shifted. Storefronts turned to carryouts and corner stores with flickering signs. The streets narrowed; the pavement grew rougher.

"So?" I asked, observing his jaw flexed as he focused on the road ahead. "Where are we headed?"

"Way-East" was his only reply.

Way-East. On the opposite side of town. And for me, a completely unfamiliar territory.

From what I remembered, Way-East and Down Bottom were

synonymous with the neighborhoods they called "Tha' Burrows." I could almost hear Mark's constant monologue as he spoke passionately about the areas formed after the Crustacean Protection Act. He could ramble on about it for hours. Let him tell it, he was basically born on the water, and when the city made his family's livelihood illegal. This place was born.

I watched in silence as the city softened and sharpened. I also noticed how easily he moved around. It all felt familiar, like this whole stretch of town expected him. So they left the porch light on.

We turned the corner where weeds pushed through cracked pavement as we continued on the crumbled asphalt. These streets had seen much better days.

We slowed and then parked at the corner building with a faded awning, its wide front windows steaming from the inside.

He sat back for a moment, looking like maybe it was something heavy on his mind. I brushed the side of his hand, and his jaw relaxed. Turning to me, he said, "Ayana, this is my grandmother's place, and" before he could finish, Ali and Skylar came bursting onto the scene, joking and laughing loud enough to completely shift the energy.

The door chimed faintly when we stepped inside.

The warm, undeniable aroma of cornbread, fried fish, and freshly baked goods greeted us and wrapped around my shoulders like a blanket of security, reclaiming the calm Skylar and Ali had interrupted just moments before.

Deep brown booths lined the walls, with some people still seated, sharing conversations and laughs. The pale yellow walls were covered in fading photographs, some signed, some framed, some neighborly black faces wearing their Sunday best.

The hostess glanced at Eli with a smile, gesturing for him to head to the back, and we followed him past the dining area toward the back, where a door sat mostly ignored. No sign, no handle, just chipped paint and a faint hum pressing from the other side. Eli grimaced in his brother's direction before he gave a light knock, pushing open the door.

Then the sound cautioned but welcomed me all at once, a pulse, thick and steady, the extra beat sitting between the last two in each measure, like the slightly off-beat thud of a murmured heart. The sound was almost wild. Voices chopped, looped, woven into the cracks now formed as instruments of their own. A battle cry of the unheard. This sound was so familiar and healing that it felt like a prayer. I was hearing the forgotten signature sound of Nevermore's music.

We traveled down a staircase that emptied into a long, stretched and dim hallway, but the walls were glowing.

Floor to ceiling on both sides was made entirely of glass. Massive in-wall aquariums that turned the corridor into a deep-sea dive. Ripples cast across the floor like reflections of water. Fish drifted past as we continued in stride. Then I caught it out of the corner of my eye. Quickly stopping in disbelief, I refocused. Like I imagined it.

A Chesapeake Blue Crab.

Perched on a rock, half-hidden behind a curtain of seaweed, with its shell a rich indigo, legs tipped in fire red. It sat there still, like it knew it was seen. Like it had something to say.

The hallway opened into a dimly lit room. Low, pulsing lights beat like a second heartbeat beneath the surface. The music is now much clearer, pouring out of weathered speakers. From the back, a red glow cast long shadows across the concrete floor. In the center, like an altar, sat an oversized stainless steel pot on a black pedestal, still warm, its sides streaked with steam and salt.

I couldn't believe it. I had only heard of places like this. Now here in the flesh, I was standing inside the infamous Shell Joint.

These establishments, secret seafood houses, were created out of sorrow and despair, and they operated completely underground.

The walls breathed history.

Wood-paneled, tagged with graffiti, a lost art, and hand-scrawled notes from nights gone by.

Behind the counter, she moved with calm authority. A dark, smooth-skinned woman, her long, loc'd hair merely drops to her knees. Her arms adorned with tribal tattoos, with eleven sixteenth-inch gauge tunnels in each ear, and those same pale gray eyes as Ali. Her body draped with a deep plum apron, her bracelets clinked as she plated food with one hand and waved off nonsense with the other.

She looked up just once, caught Eli's eye, then mine.

"Bibi," Eli started, in a much softer tone than I'd heard from him till now, "This is Ayana; Ayana, my grandmother Bibi."

"Just Yah-Yah," I said, extending my hand.

She took it with a smile. Her gaze held, not searching, knowing. Then she simply said one word.

"Come."

Ali greeted his grandmother, introducing Skylar, while hugging the slim woman like he hadn't seen her in at least a year's time.

Bibi motioned for us to sit at a table placed far right of the bar. Eli glanced at the table, then back to her, inquiring, "How did you know it would be four?"

Without missing a beat, she replied, "Know? It's not my job to know; it's my job to be ready, child."

We sat around the table, and just moments later, she returned with two platters, placing them in the center. She looked at me. "Crab cakes." Simple, like a prayer. Then, she offered a thin smile, like she could barely contain a hidden joke.

The taste, nothing short of amazing, crisp on the outside, but the inside was soft, rich, and full of a flavor I couldn't quite name. It tasted... sacred.

Skylar leaned forward, eyes wide. "This. Is what love tastes like," she said, half joking, but fully serious, before taking another bite with closed eyes.

I laughed, but totally agreed. My attention turned to Eli now. "So, were you worried about what I'd think of this place? A Shell Joint." I asked, remembering the heated exchange between him and Ali.

Remembering, he replied with a single nod.

"I'll go wherever you take me," I assured. His stern stare softened into a smile.

Bibi didn't hover as we ate...she let the food speak, and continued her normal routine in the background.

It wasn't long before we were all joking and laughing like we had done this a hundred times before.

Ali jerked as if he had forgotten something urgent, muttering something before scurrying to the exit. Skylar called after him, but she shrugged and didn't bother to run after him.

I was taking a moment to admire the art that adorned the walls of the room, now that my stomach wasn't leading the way. Eli was at the bar, refreshing our drinks, when I noticed a quilted fabric framed and hung on the far wall. It was a bold red with black and golden thread at its seams.

It was strangely familiar.

I walked over to get a better look. I reached out. It glowed, becoming warm in my grip. A chill came rushing in, causing me to shudder. My feet became fire beneath me.

Then, with a flash, I was there, standing in a small, dark room, swallowed by heat. Orange flames licking the walls, shadows dancing seductively in the flicker. Everything felt too loud, too close. But my hands stayed at my sides, unmoving. I wasn't burning. I was watching.

The entire room now seemed to spin around me. I blinked rapidly, attempting to regain focus. The fabric, still in my hand, but now cool to my touch.

Then, the smell of him as he approached.

A light touch on my shoulder.

"You cool?" Eli asked from behind me.

I nod slowly. "Yeah, I'm good." I said, but completely unsure. "Really, I'm cool, all good."

Then, across the room, her eyes. The old woman was looking directly at me like she saw everything I just saw.

Bibi's gaze was now intercepted by Ali, rushing up to her, returning with the duffle his brother had brought him to the festival.

Taking out the drum now, showing it to his grandmother like an offering.

She beamed, "How did you get this, Ali?" she inquired, before directing a scowling look to Eli. "Well, go on. That's not a paperweight. Go show your Bibi what it can do."

He cradled the drum between his knees, gently, softly rubbing his hands across the instrument's skin.

Then, over the music already playing, as he drums with precision, the lights flicker above us. He continues to strike, at a steady force. The rhythm dancing gracefully in the air that surrounded us seemed to pull Eli and me even closer.

I could feel the pulse living inside the rhythm, and now my heartbeat mirrored each tone.

This was more than sound. There was life in each beat. Something breathing in the spaces between each slap.

She motioned for Eli and me to join her at the bar.

We sat, palms clenched together like magnets, fingers like lovers, intertwined.

Comfortable.

My eyes traveled from his, traced the line of his jaw, and landed at his chest.

The more I got to know him, something about his necklace, to me, felt out of place. "You know?" my eyes, now back on his, "I noticed you really don't wear any other jewelry. No watch, rings, nothing else. But every time I see you, you have this on." My hand now rested on his chest. "You don't seem like the necklace-wearing type of guy?"

He looked down, bringing his hand to the charm. "This?"

"Legacy," Bibi interjected from behind us. He frowned, now looking down. "Eli is wearing Legacy."

Eli's shoulders dropped low, eyes averted now, and I felt it. Something in him is pulling back. Her words advertised something he wasn't ready to share. Still holding the charm, now he rubbed it vigorously with his thumb like he was trying to remove a stain.

For a second, it felt as if he weren't sitting beside me anymore. Like he ran somewhere I couldn't follow.

I studied the rise and fall of his chest as the pacing got slower.

"It was his father's," Still answering for him like I had asked her directly. "and his grandfather's before him. Eli is following in powerful footsteps." At that you'd think she'd be beaming. But there she sat, expressionless, while her grandson looked like the weight on his shoulders might take a tumble.

"Then I guess... heavy is the head that wears this crown?" Stroking his forearm, but still looking at her.

"Fact," he replied in a whisper.

Her eyes still on me, "You," not stopping even to let the drum breathe. "Where are your people from?" she asked.

Skylar shot me a comforting glance from afar.

My...People.

That question hit me like a brick to the chest.

I was a tree with missing roots.

And out of all the questions she could ask, this one made me feel like a child, defenseless.

What was she even asking? Not everyone could boast about a rich legacy, now could they? "My father," I paused, almost forgetting to breathe, "is from here, a descendant of one of Nevermore's founding families." Now breathing slower, "And my mother, New Orleans."

"His name?" her eyes narrow

"Logan." I answered slowly. "Logan Carrol."

"And your mother?"

I took a deep breath. "Adele...Broussard."

And at that she showed surprise. Softly repeating "Broussard" with a nod.

The rhythm did its best to come between us. She, now acknowledging its presence, focused on the drum. Then back to me.

"Everything started with the drum." Bibi pressed her hand to her chest, tapping out a slow, steady rhythm, as if she was calling something sacred into the room.

"Before we had language, we had rhythm," she continued. "The heartbeat shaped how we spoke. It traveled across mountains, across waters, and it was our people who knew how to listen," she smiled, remembering.

"From the call of the drum, warriors knew when to fight. Families knew when to gather.

The drum showed us when to celebrate. The drum told us when to mourn." Tapping her chest, her rhythm quickened.

"Through the drum we talked to God," she continued as her tone darkened. "Then they took us, chained us. Tried to silence us. Our drums, they destroyed, but they couldn't touch the rhythm."

Her voice strengthened, pride weaving through the pain.

"So we made our voices into drums… through song. We made our bodies drums…through dance. We carried our memories in the beat. We spoke our pain through rhythm. The drum became our guardian, our survival." She leaned forward.

"During the civil rights era, our feet marched in time, hands clapped, voices rose. Even without drums, we carried the rhythm within us.

We carried the rhythm through bebop, through jazz, through hip hop, our drums…still talking." Bibi smiled.

"James Brown said, 'Everything is a drum,' your hands, your feet, your breath, all of it.

Took us from everything we knew, everything we loved, gave us their religion to behave, and the drum refused to be silent.

It never stops reminding us.

And the beat goes on.

And you don't stop.

That's not just music you hear my grandson playing.

You hear resistance. You hear the words we speak when our words were stolen.

You hear hope.

You hear love.

You hear it because it is inside you, mon amour."

6

KEEPER OF THE FLAME
(Eli)

Alone in the deep stillness of my study, sitting only with my thoughts. The surrounding walls held more secrets than shelves, but tonight, none of them spoke louder than the truth I kept postponing.

First, I saw her and wanted to meet her.

When I met her, I knew I needed her.

Now that I have her, I can't imagine a moment that doesn't have her at my side.

But wanting her doesn't change what I am, and what I am… doesn't come with instructions.

What *I* am is as ancient as time.

Not a gift, and not a curse.

Just bound.

Bonded to memory, blood, to power.

So, I found a way to contain it. To channel it. To profit from what might have otherwise consumed me.

I deal in memory. Transactional, ancestral, sacred memories.

Relics. Not artifacts. Not antiques.

A relic is a fragment of power, sealed in an object anchored in memory. They aren't always pretty. Not always safe. But they are always, alive. They are not just magical; they're emotional. Grief can bind one. So can rage. So can love, unrequited.

People think relics are rare. They're not.

What's rare is someone who knows how to hold one without it holding them.

Relics don't whisper. They pull.

And if you don't know what you're doing, they'll pull you straight into destruction.

That's why people come to me.

People come to me to forget. To remember, conquer, destroy, to heal.

And for the right price, I can make anything yours.

I built this syndicate in silence. Silence as quiet as grief, and as deliberate as revenge. Every unit, every patron, every whisper, vetted by oath, not loyalty.

Loyalty bends, and you can teach it.

Oath is bond. You must choose it.

My clients...are sent, summoned. You can't just walk through the door. But those desperate enough to slip through the cracks of this city to find me have nothing to lose.

What they want always seems simple. But memories never are. Memories stain. Some fade. Some fight back.

I repurpose memories so that I won't become one.

Some clients trade in futures. Others trade on faith. I deal with what they thought they buried. And depending on the price, I can dig it up, or bury it deeper.

This is more than business. This is a system of need. A network of loss, want, and silence. These vices are historical. I just built the surrounding architecture. Gave it shape. Gave it rules. And for anyone who crossed me or refused to obey, I had my monster.

My monster had control over what I couldn't.

The Obayifo.

Obayifo is not a title. It's not something you can earn.

It passes through the blood, like a sickness.

No, I didn't choose this.

It chose me long before I was born.

Before I ever learned to command it, I had to learn to live with it.

They love to call us vampires, but they couldn't be more wrong. As my grandmother, Bibi, says, "Simple minds crave categories." We don't belong in any of theirs.

We don't feed on blood.

We feed beneath it.

We feed on life. Not blood, but essence.

Breath, energy, the thing that makes something alive. We don't just take; we drain souls. Around us, plant life dies. Leaves curl, flowers wilt, even the air feels off. Life can sense us, even before we speak.

The elders would say we walk with one foot in shadow, the other in flesh. My duality.

In the shadows, I learned how to track the invisible. How to smell out fear and taste lies. In the flesh, I'm a successful entrepreneur. I own a nightclub with my twin brother, and I also own the apartment complex where we reside.

If you're wondering where me, my monster and I draw the line.

I don't draw the line.

I erased it.

I deal in need.

And the girls are the most needed thing of all.

I don't take them for who they are. I take them for what they carry. They are the most valuable relics of all, and I place them where they'll get noticed.

Hunted.

*The girl with the black peeling nail polish had cuts across
her forearms where she'd tried to dig the relic out herself.
Said it whispered to her in someone else's voice. She
screamed even after I shut the door.*

I find the relics hidden in their scars and pull them forward.

*The ten-year-old with the dreams she didn't understand
She'd draw symbols in the corners of every paper scrap she
could find. Dead language. The relic within her stirred
when she slept.*

Some of them I teach.

*Jasmine bled from her eyes the night her relic fought back.
It took her voice. But before the bleeding, she asked me: "If
this is power, why does it feel like drowning?" I told her
drowning is only panic when you don't know how to
breathe underwater.*

Others I sacrificed.

* * *

The girl in the white dress. Her power surfaced with fear.
And I frightened her. Her hands sparked. Her eyes pleaded.
She reached for me. I didn't reach back.

When they can't wield it, I will. This kind of power comes with a large price tag.

But somehow, I had missed *her* power.

Ayana.

I felt an immediate attraction at first sight.

I realized she was masked when I stood outside her shop. Someone has hidden her abilities. They've gone to drastic measures to protect her from people like me.

Still, *she* found *me*.

Now we have something between us that no one can deny.

I saw how she reacted to the relics at the museum and at Bibi's. She doesn't even know her own power.

So how do I keep her and tell her the truth about me?

Who I am.

What I do.

Why *should* she stay?

I invited her to my club.

If I'm going to tell her the truth, it has to be in my domain.

7

INTO THE FIRE
(Yah-Yah)

I went through my closet in a whirlwind, not knowing what to wear. After all, was this a date? Either way, I had to impress. Eventually, I settled on an elegant off-the-shoulder, puffy-sleeved crop top, paired with a geo-print, high-split maxi skirt, matching clutch, and open-toe heels. I pulled my locs into a high bun, applied a natural beat, and generously applied a vanilla fragrance. Honestly, I wasn't sure what to expect, but Eli's driver, Roderick, picked me up at 9 o'clock sharp, as promised.

When we pulled up at Flux, I couldn't believe my eyes. I was witnessing paradise right on the docks of Nevermore. Somehow, this club felt like a luxurious resort, built on heat, rhythm, and fantasy. Inside pulsed with beautiful, bright colors, and heat that radiated from minimally attired bodies that left very little to imagine.

Ali stood behind the booth, center stage.

The music? Infectious.

It was like a spell spilled into the atmosphere.

Melody moving across my skin and lingering at my hips.

I'd been nervous all day thinking about seeing Eli tonight. It's been days since we were together, though we speak on the phone constantly.

Searching for a brief calm before the inevitable impending storm, I spotted the bar far left and almost sprinted in its direction, before, like a vision, he appeared.

Drink in hand extended to me.

Standing in off-white slim-fit textured slacks, a matching short-sleeved v-neck polo clung to his chest, and brown laced loafers made his outfit complete. His locs were pulled together neatly in a high bun.

"Ayana, you made it," he smiled. Smelling like bergamot and a soft white musk, "Come in so I can show you around."

He took a moment.

Letting his eyes drift over every inch of me before directing his attention to the stage. "You see DJ Pain in the ass up there? My younger, much less handsome, but very talented brother," he said, laughing from his gut. "There's something different to show you in every room."

I trailed him closely into a dimly lit space, with a stage in its center. Beautiful women wearing vivid bright colors moved seductively on the elevated surface. Every surrounding chair was full, but he, without a hint of alarm, gently grabbed my hand, guiding us to a sectioned-off area.

We sat on a plush couch. The infectious music still played from the main stage in smaller speakers within the room.

Now, with my attention on the stage, I realized how wrong I'd been. The women dancing weren't just barely dressed; they were stark naked.

Just painted in fluorescent colors that glowed in the dark. More of them sprinkled throughout the small crowd. Before I could even comment, one of the beautiful women came and straddled and began grinding on top of him. Unmoved, he motioned for her to get up.

She did.

Then, closing the space between us, she grazed a delicate, vanilla-scented hand across my face, blowing me a kiss; her finger lingered right at my lips.

My cheeks warmed instantly. I laughed it off, even though my shoulders tightened.

"So, this is what you bring all your guests to see?"

He looked at me, unreadable.

"Only the ones worth bringing, Ayana," he said.

Now fully flustered, not expecting that at all, my heart stuttered. I hated how easy it was to fall under his spell.

He rose and guided me to the exit.

The next room felt more intimate.

Dim red light lit the velvet walls. An electric avant-garde jazz trio soothed the space with sharp notes and lazy rhythm, almost slurred, fractured, but still in sync. The keyboard and bass stood on either side of the drummer, who had no sticks, no cymbals, just a classic drum machine, his hands effortlessly tapping out a drunken cadence.

The air in here was less intense. Slower.

The room, lined with velvet booths and deep armchairs, low tables scattered around the stage. A bar sat in the far corner. Eli stood behind me silently, so close I could feel his body heat. Watching me take it all in.

We stepped to the bar.

"Mr. Osei," a slim Hispanic gentleman greeted Eli from behind the bar. "Your usual, I presume?" Eli replied with a simple nod.

"And for you, beautiful?" the bartender asked. His eyes said much more.

"For her, a Blood Orange Sazerac. Adrián," Eli quickly replied

I raised a brow.

Did I sense a tinge of jealousy in his tone? Now Eli's eyes were carving into him from over the bar. I was tempted to be playful at this moment, but I behaved. It was no time to antagonize him.

"What's in it?" I gently stroked his forearm. Knowing exactly how to simmer his flame.

"Miss Broussard." His eyes on mine, "Magic." He smirked. "And a little patience."

Our drinks were placed in front of us now. I slowly sipped.

The drink burned, then bloomed, like he did.

"You look incredible tonight." He leaned in. "I'm glad you came."

We sat in that for a moment, just enjoying the space of each other's company.

He stood, placing his empty glass down. "There's still much more to see."

We left the velvet room and slipped into a narrow corridor lined with full-length mirrors.

As we walked, I glanced at the two of us reflected.

With my hand in his, our outfits perfectly complemented each other as we walked in sync. The music from the next room pulsed through the corridor.

Stepping into the cool blue-lit room, scented vapor hung thick in the air. The music flowed slow and sensual.

The booths in this room were low and plush. Curtains hung from the ceiling at each booth. Some pulled shut.

Bodies danced against other bodies all around us.

I turned to him. He placed his hand on my lower back. Activating the movement that flowed freely from my spine.

I pulled him closer to me.

He gripped me tighter.

Looking at him. Everything around me vanished.

Almost.

Then I heard it.

Steady thuds, muffled moans.

Drawn by sound and instinct, I glanced through a half-open curtain.

A girl with platinum curls was riding a dark-skinned man, her body arching like a wave, spine curling like a serpent. His head thrown back, hands gripping her waist, guiding every rise and fall.

I gasped.

My chest heaved.

My feet tingled beneath me. Then the world shifted.

Suddenly, I wasn't just watching.

I was there. On top.

Hands braced against the booth.

With his hands guiding me, my body moved like it already knew the rhythm.

It was electric. And wrong.

I didn't know how to stop it.

His damp, heavy hand gripped my face as his thrusts slowed, pressing deeper, both of us trembled.

Then Eli's palm found my cheek.

Gentle. Grounding.

My breath snapped back into me.

He blinked.

I lightly pull away, ashamed like he could see my thoughts.

Like he heard them but didn't say a word.

Just studied me.

His thumb brushed along my cheek, slow and thoughtful, like he was memorizing something fragile.

I forced a laugh. Too light. "I think that drink hit harder than I expected." But my voice betrayed me. I was still inside whatever that was.

Now the music held me like a deep embrace.

His eyes spoke. Only to me.

I was. Safe.

The silence settled between us like velvet. One hand still warm on my lower back. Around us, the room throbbed with bodies and smoke. But it was like we were inside a pause.

"Come on," he said finally, his fingers brushing softly against mine. "One more room."

I let him lead me, glad for the excuse to move, even if my legs felt frozen.

Still wearing the heat of the club around me, I sobered with the evening's cool air as we stepped into the evening air. The view of the city was beautiful from here.

The rooftop area held a shallow reflective pool in its center, framed with plush daybeds surrounded by sheer curtains flowing seductively in the night's air.

Removing our shoes. We sank into the deep cushions. Silently. Facing each other. Enjoying a shared communication with the breeze.

A slim, muscular gentleman was hugged in beige linen fabric. His chest was bare to the elements as he advanced towards us. His eyes averted from mine as he handed us champagne glasses filled to the rim.

Eli smiled. Dismissing him with a nod.

With slow sips, I took in my surroundings. We were in the company of a few couples, enjoying their separate conversations.

Placing my glass on the low table in front of us, I rose. Knotting my skirts bottom so it now stopped at my knees.

I walked to the pool and stepped inside the cool water. Eli stood scanning the company that surrounded us. He approached, now standing facing me at the pool's edge. The water, stopping at my calf, chilled by the night. Our palms met, igniting that feeling from our night at the museum.

"You ever come up here alone" I asked, shifting as the water rippled around me.

"I do", he replied with a smile. "But it's much better with company" we both stood, front facing as the air caressed the air we shared.

With the temperature on a steady upward climb, "Eli, I think maybe I should go. "

He glanced at the water's surface as if he needed to prepare for a sudden fall. "I can have my driver take you back whenever you like."

Then, quietly, I scanned his expression before my reply. "I was thinking maybe," my palms slipped to both sides of his belt. "I was thinking maybe you'd come with me."

Eyes locked on mine, he said, "Let's stop at my office so I can grab my keys."

Eli said nothing else. He just took my hand.

We left the rooftop in silence, the night following us like a second skin. The music from inside softened behind us, replaced by the soft hum of the elevator descending.

Down one floor, the hallway changed. Sleek, dim, quieter. Eli keyed in a code, and the heavy double doors to his office opened with a soft click.

He reached for my hand to lead me inside. I paused long enough to catch a flicker of hesitation in his eyes.

Before I could overthink it, I grabbed his belt and pulled him closer.

Without missing a beat, he kissed me so deeply I almost lost balance, but quickly recovered before pressing him into the doorway frame. Ripping open his slacks.

I dropped to my knees. Drew him in slowly, and softly sang to his soul, causing him to moan obscenities...until I swallowed, sonnets. The moan in his throat was half prayer and half curse.

One hand wrapped around my neck. In a fluid motion, he pulled me up, guiding me inside, pressing me against the wall as the doors closed behind us.

Eli kissed me like he'd been waiting a lifetime. Two heartbeats, composed within the same song.

He kneeled in front of me like I was something sacred. My lips folded into his. He tasted me like he was starving.. I fed him until I could no longer stand. He stood and held me softly.

Guiding us deeper into the room, he steadied me on his desk. When he hovered on top of me, I swear I saw light shimmer from behind him. Like something unspoken that finally found its voice. It wrapped around us while he loved me slowly, looking deep in my eyes. His eyes asked questions, like, "Can I trust you? Do you feel safe here?" My body sternly asked for more. Not allowing my soul to answer.

I reversed my position, gripping each side of the desk while steadying my gaze straight ahead. I let out a primal grunt as he barged in from behind, grabbing my hair as he gripped my waist and pushed until his flesh was against my flesh.

I begged.

He granted.
I gave.
He took.
I pulled.
He pushed.
And
We…
fulfilled.
I asked him never to lie to me.
He promised he couldn't
I asked him not to leave me tonight
He promised he wouldn't.
We choreographed life's movement until time forgot itself and only we remained. Flesh, passion, our souls bound.

******

I woke up still wearing the warmth of his skin. Still wrapped in black satin sheets. The lights were dim. The air, warm.

I clung to him.

My cheek was against his chest, my bare skin laid against his.

Maybe I should feel embarrassed. But without shame, I pressed myself closer.

I felt seen. Claimed.

I traced my finger along his chest as he slept, then gently reached for the crescent moon he hadn't taken off.

It felt familiar.

Strange.

I was there again.

That damp, dark place.

This time it felt bigger.

Symbols glowed on the walls. Girls scattered across the space.

Scared.

I trembled.

He looked like Eli, but not exactly.

Not older. Just different. Sharper.

His golden eyes burned with hatred. They stared straight through me.

His hands rose, summoning something from the shadows.

The floor pulsed beneath me.

I tried to move. Tried to scream. Tried to wake up.

Then I gasped.
My body jerked.
I was back.
Back in his arms. In Eli's bed.
Still wrapped in black satin. Still pressed against his chest.
Except now he was wide awake.
Staring at me.
Those eyes couldn't possibly hold danger. Could they?
Those eyes had made promises my body begged for.
They couldn't have seen what I just saw.
That had to be a dream.
But what was this necklace?
Why hadn't he taken it off?
Pushing those questions out of my mind, I clung to him even tighter.
I needed to leave.
I wanted to stay.

8

FANNING THE FLAMES
(Eli)

I was lying alone and naked, with the smell of her vanilla perfume still fresh on my skin, and the silk sheets clinging to my body the way she left it. The room is warm, but not enough to explain the heat still curled in my chest.

The pillow still held an indent where she had lain. I drag my fingers across silk, searching for the warmth from her, but she's gone. I swear I can still feel the press of her thigh on mine, causing my body to react. Still heavy from the weight of her.

I try to close my eyes, but it's worthless. The room remembers her. Silk sheets wrinkled, yearning for her. These walls. My skin.

It's better that she's gone. A clean break.

But that's not true. I almost died the moment I entered her. Now I'm trying desperately to hold on. Last night I felt it shift. Tasting her need while pressing her against the wall. On top of her, on my desk. Still, she touched me like she meant it. It was like she saw me. Not just the man, but the thing underneath. And she didn't run.

Not then, at least.

But this morning, she touched the pendant.

And her eyes were full of questions she didn't ask.

Before she left, I knew I should've stopped her. Said something. Explained. But what would I say?

64

Should I have said what she touched wasn't just jewelry? That my grandmother gave me this necklace after the fire?

Could I have told her it's older than me, older than this city, soaked in the screams of my parents I couldn't save?

I sit up, elbows on my knees, head heavy in my hands. The pendant dangles from my neck, brushing against my chest like it's trying to remind me who I am.

What had she seen? How much of it did she know was real? I don't know how much of it reached her, but I felt her pulse change the second her fingers grazed the crescent. Felt her energy stutter. For a moment, I knew something had tugged her away.

I want to think of her like she's just another girl, and this was just a night full of lust. But the way she looked at me last night... I should've let it burn. Should've pulled away before she could reach in that far. But I didn't.

Because a broken part of me wanted her to see. Wanted her to know. Wanted to be known.

I pull myself out of bed. Walking into the bathroom, I rush to the mirror, half hoping she's still in the reflection.

Just me.

This face.

These scars.

My eyes.

And the monster that stood there waiting.

The pendant glows faintly, as if her touching it left something behind. It's like it remembers her, too.

She left before the truth could find her.

But it will.

And when it does, I don't know if she'll still look at me like she wants me.

Or if she'll run.

******

I stepped into my baby brother's domain for a change of scenery. He didn't flinch when I opened the door. Just leaned back deeper into the couch, arm draped across the top like a throne. His eyes looked up slowly, sharply. Like he'd been waiting.

Not surprised.

Not warm.

Nor was he unkind. Just… watching.

That calm, unreadable look he wore when he was about to cut through the bullshit. This look made it clear he already knew something I hadn't seen yet.

"Boy, you smell like good lovin' and endless regret," he joked.

Stepping into my brother's place was like walking into a whole other world.

No shadows lived here.

Glass and chrome reflected the morning light from every angle, bouncing off the white marble floors that looked untouched. The air was cool, almost cold. Not a single pillow out of place, not a single object without purpose. Everything about the space was intentional, precise.

"Ali, chill. I'm fresh out of the shower, so I know I smell like a classic man." Plopping down on the sofa beside him, "And when have u known this man to regret?"

"Shiiiiit," he laughed, giving me a playful shove. "I thought you'd still be laid up with shorty right now. But she's gone. And you just let her leave?"

His question hung between us. I knew he could feel it. Some of what I was carrying, even if I hadn't said a word.

"It was nothing, Ali. Got some amazing head and a quick fuck in my office. A little too quick." I adjusted myself, palm resting low. "Brought her back here for seconds. Had to blow out her back just to drain the rest of it from my system."

Ali leaned in, eyes narrowing. "That's a hell of a story for a man who looks to have lost more than pride coming up short in the first round. What aren't you saying, Eli?"

I shifted, trying hard to avoid that knowing gaze. "Ali, it really is nothing." The words tasted bitter on my tongue. "Though the way she pulled the devil out of me with her tongue is definitely enough to keep her on speed dial."

He smirked. "You don't look like a man who's convinced himself of that. You're off. What's really going on?"

I ran a hand through my locs, letting them fall wild, tension tight in my chest. "It's… Yah-Yah, Ali. She's different. Messed with my head more than I expected."

Ali's smirk faded, replaced by something sharper. "Oh, my big brother, definitely getting a little soft. You losing your edge?"

I shook my head. "No. But I'm not used to this. Not used to someone seeing more of me, not just the man, but the rest of it."

He leaned back, arms crossed. "You'd better be careful. Getting too tangled means losing control. You know what happens when you lose control."

I swallowed, voice low. "I know."

Ali's eyes flickered. "There's more, isn't there? You're not telling me something about what happened last night?"

I hesitated. "Maybe."

"What did you let her see?" he asked.

I looked away. "Brother, you don't wanna know."

He leaned forward, voice low but firm. "Try me."

The room felt smaller with his eyes on me. I swallowed hard. "She touched the relic around my neck. The one I never take off. And when she did, something changed. She saw something... something I've been trying to keep buried."

Ali's expression softened. "That thing you carry around like a damn weight."

I nodded, feeling the truth settle heavy in the air between us.

"And what happened? Did she freak out? Run? Or did she actually stick around?"

I ran a hand over my face, tired. "She stayed. Even after. But she was a little unsure."

He shook his head, a half-smile tugging at his lips. "This could either break you or be the start of something."

I scoffed. "I'm not sure which one I want more."

Ali's eyes flicked toward the window. "Well, whatever happens, don't let it swallow you whole.

9

SLOW BURN
(Yah-Yah)

The warm water softly caressed my skin, thick steam curling around me like smoke. I closed my eyes, letting my thoughts drift to him. His scent still lingered in the air. The memory of his touch stayed close.

My fingers moved on their own, soft and slow, following the lines where he had held me. The heat inside me stirred, raw and electric, pulling me deeper into a memory I was not ready to let go of.

The water traced every curve, slipping down my shoulders and back. My locs soaked through until they hung heavy down my spine. The rhythm of the drops matched the pulse beneath my skin. It felt like a quiet drumbeat that mirrored the rhythm of his body against mine.

One hand pressed against the tile as I remembered him on my skin. The other found the heat still burning for him. It was not just desire. It was something heavier. I traced slow circles along the places he had touched.

He was hard to ignore.

Now drenched in a mix of want and something darker, I felt it rise. A warning, quiet and low, whispered just beneath the surface.

The water rinsed away the sweat and tension. It could not reach the part of me that still screamed for him.

I closed my eyes and let the steam carry me back to the way he looked at me. There was the man. And there was the monster. Both

68

lived in one gaze. I pressed harder, trying to calm the storm inside.

I stepped out of the shower slowly, letting the air cool his heat on my skin. The towel holding me close in his absence.

Before I oiled my skin or put on clothes, I stood there… listening.

The house was still. No music, T.V., no whistle from a teakettle. Just silence stretching around me like a question I didn't want answers to.

I pressed my fingers to my lips. I could still taste him.

He was still here. Not in body, but everywhere.

I glimpsed at my reflection walking past my bedroom mirror. Bare, damp, marked. My neck, my thighs, all signed by him.

I turned away from the mirror and reached for the coconut oil on my dresser.

Rubbing it between my palms, then across my arms, legs, shoulders.

I was desperate to feel normal again. But every glide of my hands reminded me of his.

I pulled on a maxi skirt, white tank and a pair of sneakers. No makeup. No earrings. Headwrap, low over my damp locs.

Today wasn't for doing too much.

Today I was just trying to breathe.

Inside the rideshare, the city passed in a blur. Neon signs still blinked from the night before. Corner stores pulling up their gates. Everything is in motion. Except me.

My thoughts were still tangled in sheets, staring out the window.

By the time we pulled up to the shop, I still hadn't shaken him off.

Inside, Skylar glared at me.

"Damn, you good Yanni?" she said, voice full of concern but laced with urgency.

"I'm cool. Just exhausted."

"Green juice waiting on your sta—" she stopped. Her eyes sharpened.

"No. No. Wait, bitch, because I've known you longer than I've known myself."

She stepped from behind the counter. "Ayana… come here." Now she was looking me up and down. "You walking up in here like you got in some good trouble," grabbing my chin. "Ayana!"

"What Sky!" I pulled away, now annoyed.

"You fucked him, didn't you?!?"

My silence answered for me.

"Well, why you come up in here like you needed an exorcism instead of a good nut?"

At that, I chuckled.

Knowing this talk was not avoidable I joined her at the bar. "I know this is a fucking Q & A, but make it quick so we can open."

Placing a green juice in front of me, "So yesterday you went to Flux, right? I passed through to check out Ali, but I had a gig too."

I sipped, "Yeah, I went to the club."

Sky raised an eyebrow. "Okay, well we don't have all day. Where did this go down?"

I hesitated, taking another sip. Didn't answer fast enough.

Her eyes widened. "Wait. Wait. Don't tell you... Yanni you fucked him in the club!?!"

"His.... Office," I whispered, "at first."

Sky slapped the counter. "At first?! Girl, what the hell does that mean?"

I groaned, dropping my head into my hands. "It means I made it worse. Better. I don't know."

She leaned in, grinning now. "Now you know. And I want every damn detail, but I will take the cliff notes virgin right now." Whispering now, "Was it good?"

I looked down. "Sky." Biting my bottom lip with closed eyes.

She froze, mouth falling open. "That good?"

I nodded once, slowly. "So good..."

"Like fuck em again good?"

"Yes, but Sky. It was just that... a fuck, no strings."

Sky gave me a long, flat look. "Yanni, you don't look like someone who got no strings attached. Your ass look wrapped tied and tangled to me."

I sighed. "I needed it. He needed it. That's all it was. Nothing serious."

She tilted her head, studying me. "You sure? Because you came in here like you had just been with the ghost of Dickmas Past."

I didn't answer. Just sipped my juice.

"Uh huh," she muttered. "No strings, my ass. And get ur ass together before Titi gets here and gets all in ur ass about it."

I headed for my station, forcing my mind past the subject of him. Sky was right. I didn't need to attract Titi's concern.

I wiped down my chair, sprayed the combs, and lined up the products. Busy hands, quiet thoughts. Or so I hoped, cause even as I sectioned and twisted coils, I could feel him. This shit was like a song stuck in the back of my throat. An unforgettable melody that I couldn't get out of my head.

At this point, my movements were muscle memory. Drape. Wash. Re-twist. Dryer. Style. Like clockwork. Again and again. Occasional small talk, but I was on a mission to get home to sleep away this feeling.

By the time the last client left, my feet ached and my back was tight. The shop had quieted down; the hum of hood dryers had long faded.

Skylar's boyfriend Mark had shown up, apparently unexpectedly, and his surprise appearance visibly irritated her. Even in her irritation, he was so attentive to her. Wiping down the bar in her place, assisting with our routine clean up.

Afterward, he began helping her gather her belongings.

I was wiping down my station slowly, the motions steady, deliberate. Watching Mark dote on an aloof Skylar. Adjusting her hoodie at her waist, he placed her signature headphones over her head and placed a simple kiss on her brow as she gazed up at him.

I told them both to leave ahead of me.

I needed time to just clear my head.

******

A warm bath and a night of undisturbed sleep were what I craved. I needed him out of my system; I didn't have time for this type of distraction. Still, I felt plagued by the unsettling feeling that I needed, but didn't need him all at once. I pulled the shop door closed, and as I turned the key, I thought about being wrapped in his caramel complexion.

I wanted him so badly I could actually smell his cologne.

Then.

I felt his grip on my wrist.

It was really him, pulling me closer to him and kissing the top of my forehead.

"What are you doing here?" I asked softly.

He led me to the adjacent alley. Darkness, and the smell of oil and pavement surrounded us. The night breeze brushed over my skin. With urgency, he backed me into the brick, reaching under my skirt and pushing the thin barrier to the side.

Gripping my hips, he lifted me effortlessly. Pushing himself inside. No prep, no mercy, just pure hunger. My back scraped against the brick wall. This time, I knew I saw light radiating from behind him and surrounding us. I gripped his hair as he plunged deeper inside, with my legs melting around him. Dug my nails deep into his flesh. His growling in my ear, complemented by my breathy moans performed over the sounds of our bodies slapping together, was the soundtrack of my desire. His eyes glowed like embers burning inside. He placed a hand over my mouth to stifle my screams. Growling as his body froze, his grip around me tightened. Then, for a moment, we yielded.

I stayed still in his arms, against the wall. The weight of this silence held us both captive. His forehead rested on mine. His sweats were still at his ankles.

My skirt clinging to my wet thighs.

I couldn't look at him. Not yet.

"Ayana…" he finally said, voice low, unsure.

I shook my head. "Don't." I knew that this thing we had wasn't over. But I needed time before I let it become anything more. "Just take me home."

He nodded. No questions asked. Just us getting adjusted in the dark. We walked out of the alley as if nothing had happened.

I peeled off my clothes the second I stepped through the door, letting each piece fall wherever it landed.

No shower, I would just wear him on me till morning, my bare skin comforted in the cool sheets. I search the ceiling as if I'd find clarity there.

No luck; instead, I drifted to sleep.

The dark room felt endless. Symbols glowed on the walls. Girls scattered across the space. I was there. Those eyes that looked like his. A girl turned and looked right at me and mouthed … Ayana.

I woke with a scream in my throat, staring again for the clarity that had never been there.

The room was spinning.

I had left him, but something left with me.

****

6:30AM

Me:

Sky, I'm not working today. Can you contact my clients?

They will have to reschedule.

I can't do this today.

* * *

6:50 AM

Sky:

Yanni you ok?

Me: I've got a lot on my mind.

I need a day to just...not think. About anything.

6:55 AM

Sky: It's gonna be okay, Yanni.

You get some rest and

I'll hit you a little later to check on ya.

Most of the night I cried, and the few moments that remained left me restless.

Helpless.

This morning, I let Skylar know I needed the day off.

I knew she'd be concerned. I just didn't have the words to explain what was wrong. Ironically, the only thing holding me together was knowing she'd have my back, no matter what the hell this was.

Last night, I could've sworn she was here. It felt like she came and calmed me down after I woke up screaming. Rocking me like a baby. Whispering that everything was going to be okay.

Today, I just wanted to sleep.

I knew better.

Closing the shop had clearly sent up a smoke signal. For me, there was no shock an hour later when I heard the lightest knock on my bedroom door before it gently creaked open.

Titi, I saw first, with a stern stare desperately trying to hide her genuine worry from creeping through. She scanned my face to determine what was wrong. Next, Skylar stepped from behind Titi timidly. Her signature headphones hung at her neck.

"Yanni, please don't be upset," Sky said, brushing my locs from my face. "I had to call her. I was worried." She climbed into the bed beside me. "Now, the first thing we're going to do is get you a…"

"Robe," Titi cut in, tossing it at me from the hook behind the door. "We've got some talkin' to do, and I ain't tryin' to have Skylar's simple ass losin' focus 'cause you over there stark-ass naked."

"Titi!" Sky covered her face with both hands.

"If I'm lying, then my ass flew here." We all chuckled.

"Yanni, it smells like sex and sympathy up in here!" she said, waving her hands in the surrounding air.

"Sky, leave her alone," she continued in a softer tone. "Now, you tell your Titi what's really going on."

I exhaled.

"I don't really know how to explain." My eyes locked on the fingers of my right hand as I fidgeted with the ring on my pointer.

Titi forged through the heavy silence, now sitting opposite to Skylar by my side. Her eyes locked on the ring as I spun it around my finger.

For a moment, the metal appeared to glow.

I blinked, trying to push it out of my mind.

Not here, not now.

I had to get it together.

I tried to refocus, expecting the vision to disappear, but it was still there, glowing between us.

Our eyes locked.

"Feels like you're seeing what's really not there." She reached for my hand. "Feels like you're losing control when objects start moving right before your eyes. Sometimes it feels like something is calling your name." She was stroking the back of my hand held in hers.

My mouth dropped.

"I'm confused. Titi, what exactly are you telling me?"

"What I should have told you for a long time now." Her grip tightened. "You come from a line touched by ancestral magic. A gifted few, hiding in plain sight."

"Ancestral?"

"Magic, yes." She continued. "But not the way you are probably thinking 'bout it, chile." She laughed, swatting at me playfully.

"Witches? Yes, but aint no heavy robe wearin', wand wavin' and Latin shoutin'." She paused, gifting me a little time to catch up. "You were born a Protector. And what we carry is much, much heavier."

"We?"

"Protectors, yes. Guardians of relics." Titi paused, taking a moment to make sure I was following along.

"And before you go asking. Relics are things passed down through time. Ancient objects that carry power, emotion, and strength." Her tone was more serious now.

"Relics never forget. They remember every hand that ever held them. And because we are creations made to protect them, we can sense when they are near. Through visions, we can see them. When needed, they call out and pull us closer to them."

"So why didn't you tell me before now?" I asked.

It would have done so much for me to know that I was a part of something bigger, all those years when I felt so small.

Right now I was hearing all of this along with my younger self, holding her tiny hand as it trembled in mine. Everything we had experienced made more sense to us now.

I wanted to lash out. I wanted to give my aunt a piece of my mind.

But before that anger even bloomed, something pulled me into Titi's gaze.

Tears had soaked her cheeks.

I watched them travel slowly down her face as she reflected on a time when she was forced to decide.

"At first, I thought you were too young. I didn't want to put anything else on ya. Already lost so much. Instead of taking you back home with me, I thought it was easier to stay here in plain sight. Nevermore barely knows its power anymore. That made it easy to hide." My heart dropped. She stepped away from everything she had known, just to keep me safe. The silence from earlier found us again.

"So the times I felt like I was walking inside of a dream. That was because I'm a Protector?" I asked, trying to fully embrace this foreign concept.

Titi and Sky's eyes met.

Titi let out a labored breath.

"Well, Protectors are never just one thing, baby," Titi said, reaching out for my hand. I relaxed into her grip. "We each carry a different fragment of the legacy. Some are called Keepers; they hold the memories. Some are Seers; they can read energy and time and tell you what's next. And others can channel power through sounds, touch, through prayer."

She touched her chest. "Me? I'm a healer. Among many other things, I can right any relic that's tainted, wronged by ill emotions. Pull the poison out of relics, people too when it's possible. I have a special place hidden, where I sometimes do my work." She beamed with pride. "Our kind don't fight the wars, but we keep the balance. Each Protector has a purpose, just as each relic has a will. But you, Ayana. You are not only a Protector. "

My head tilted. I could barely process another revelation.

"You've got a mixed lineage, a hybrid, first of your kind. Your mother, the youngest daughter of the Broussard family. A long line of Protectors rooted in Louisiana before time even knew itself. But your father was an empath."

"So I'm both a Protector and an *Empath*?"

"That means more than sense relics. You can actually read them. They don't just tell you what they are; they show you. And when they call out to you, you can travel through time and space to get to them. So no baby. That was not a dream you were walking through. They have a name for it. They call that Soul Steppin'."

"No bullshit?" I whispered, staring at Titi through wide eyes.

Then I remembered. Those dark, empty nights when my mother was roaming the streets. The times my daddy looked lost, staring into space. He was actually *with* her.

This was too much to take in. My attention clung to my aunt now. "And I'm supposed to do what with all of this? I don't even know what it is or how to control it."

"Now I can show you everything there is about being a Protector, but I can't show you how to Soul Step or help you control that power, baby."

"If you can't…then who can?" I asked softly. Still trying to process it all.

Then, through the silence, I was hit with the unexpected in a simple whisper. Skylar spoke.

"Me," she said timidly as she brought the headphones up to cover her ears.

"No…now you keeping shit from me too, Sky?" I asked, half hurt, but mostly confused.

"Yanni, for most of my life I have been bound, to you! That means that whatever you felt, I felt." She gripped both sides of the headphones for a moment.

Now, feeling less hurt. I understood now; she wore the headphones to protect herself from being too overcome with emotion. Suddenly my heart felt heavy.

"Yeah, you feel that, huh?" My heart was racing. Hers too. I didn't know where she ended or where I began.

"For as long as I have known you, your power has been unvoiced, Yanni." She continued taking deep breaths while holding a teary gaze. "Soul Steppin' feels like reaching through your own emotions…just to cradle someone else's, so they can rest, even if it's just for a fucking moment."

"Sky…" All this time I thought she was just an amazing friend, but maybe she had been holding me up more than I'd ever given her credit.

"Tell me," she continued, "what would be the point in bringing you into something you not only hadn't experienced, but something you didn't at all understand? It wasn't until I saw you react to that quilt on the wall at the Shell Joint that I knew you had to have slipped through."

"Shell Joint?!?!?" Titi interrupted. "I know good and goddamn well my babies were not down at nobody's damn Shell Joint!" Now on her feet, both hands on her hips.

Skylar froze.

I fell silent.

Our eyes held a deeper conversation we couldn't have out loud.

"And what quilt? Why wouldn't you have told me this sooner, Skylar?" Titi was fuming. "How many times do I have to remind you that you are supposed to be looking out for her?"

"That's exactly what I've been doing."

"We can talk about it later," Titi cut Skylar off before she had a chance to even explain.

Titi was looking at me now. I felt almost like a child again, sitting beneath the weight of her judgement.

"Tell me right now, is any of this about that damn boy from the festival? With them shifty eyes and that slick city charm? He's throwing around his riches like candy off a parade float." She asked, though we were both sure she already knew the answer.

I looked at Skylar, searching for an escape route in her eyes, but she turned away.

"Titi," speaking through uncertainty, "I think. I love him." There, I said it, and it didn't feel wrong.

Titi looked like I had knocked the wind out of her. She wanted to scream from the blow. But she only whispered.

"Jesus."

10

PLAYING WITH FIRE
(Eli)

I woke up butt-ass naked, drenched in sweat. My heart pounded in my chest like I'd been shadowboxing. Sheets scattered about like I had been fighting a ghost.

Ayana.

I hadn't meant to see her again that soon, but I ran to her with urgency, like she was calling for me. Then there I was, deep inside her in an alley, like we didn't see the danger looming between us. I couldn't and wouldn't stop. A primal hunger was begging to be released, and her hips were urging me to give it all to her.

Now, it's all I can think about. The way she wouldn't look at me after. Like she was holding something in. Or keeping something out.

The way she looked at me before she turned away like she saw it. Like she knew. I kept replaying it, searching for the exact second her eyes changed. Not fear. Not exactly. But something close. Recognition maybe?

I sat up, elbows on my knees, palms pressed to my face.

Something shifted that night. Not just in her. In the air. In me.

If it were just sex, it would be easy. This would be done. But the thought of her burned inside me.

I ran my hand down my face, dragging sweat and sleep with it, trying to shake the feeling that something had passed between us. In breath, in rhythm, in blood. Not stolen. Activated.

And I don't know what she saw, but I'm certain it saw her back.

A knock at the door. I groaned.

"Yooooooo," my brother's voice, "You alive in there?"

Pulling the sheet to my lap as I glanced at the trail of clothes leading to my bed.

Ali knocked again, lighter this time. "I'm coming in." His eyes wider, "Looks like you either fucked or fought a demon up in here, Eli!"

He came closer, gaze narrowing. "You gonna tell me what's up? Bro, I've been calling you for hours."

"Ali! I'm fine!" I screamed.

"I'm assuming you forgot we were meeting Bibi? Get the fuck up and come on!"

"Then reschedule, Ali! I'm not going, can't!" The familiar fire was slowly burning behind my eyes.

"Oh, you can't? Sure, no worries, I completely understand." He paused, judging me through that pale gaze. "You selfish son of a bitch! Get up!"

"Ali, what's the big deal?"

"Is this about Ayana?" he knowingly asked before taking a seat at the foot of my bed.

"Oh, cause now you care?"

"When have I shown I don't care?"

"I told you I didn't want to take her to Bibi's. I wanted to keep her out of that part of my world. But you completely ignored me!"

"What's the big deal?" he chuckled. "A day ago, you said the two of you weren't even a thing."

I leaned back on my elbows, my eyes focused on the ceiling above me. He wasn't lying, nor was he intentionally being a jerk. Ali was just going off of what I had told him. And I knew the moment I said it, it couldn't have been further from the truth.

"Eli, you know that…you could date her, right? You deserve a normal life." He said in a much softer tone than before, "You've always had a lot on your shoulders. We wouldn't have most of our lifestyle without you. But I think you deserve a shot at something… happier."

"Happier?"

"Yes, E, happier. Maybe if you let her in…she might just understand some of what you're carrying."

"Oh, she's gonna understand that I walked through hell to come home to paradise?"

"You could try. Cause at some point, you're going to burn your whole house down trying to put out your own fire."

With that, my brother rose and exited without another word.

****

I pondered contacting her, wrestling with my apprehension. All I really wanted was to hear her voice. But I didn't want to crowd her.

I just sat alone on my sofa, staring at my phone with my thumb hovering above her name.

Then, before I could cower or talk myself out of it, I hit the button.

Two rings felt like an eternity to hear her delicate yet raspy voice on the other end.

"Hello?"

I didn't answer right away.

Just listened.

That voice, a calm to my raging storm.

"Hey you," I finally said. "I was just thinking about you."

"Hey you." She returned, "I enjoy being thought about." I could hear her smile through the line.

"What are you up to?"

"Is this like your way of asking me if I missed you, Eli?" she asked in a tone that could get anything she wanted from me.

"Shit, maybe I enjoy being thought about, too. Can't a brother get some loving up in here?"

"Maybe I was trying to forget you." She laughed lightly.

"Oh, is that right?" she never failed to flirt with my flames. "You think all of you could forget me?"

"How badly do you want to know?" She asked. "And if I tell you… what are you going to do about it?"

"I think I've already shown you I want to be wherever you are, Ayana."

"You always know what to say to move me, even though I'm trying not to budge."

"Pushy?"

"Tempting…"

"Then come tempt me." I said, both daring and pleading in the same breath.

"You can't always get what you want whenever you want it, Eli."

"Well, do you want to?" I asked her.

She responded with a brief silence before saying, "Sometimes, things you want have consequences. Cool it,"

"Alright, but I'm about to go for a swim. What are the odds that you'll join me?"

"That's tempting, but-"

"My driver's outside; see you soon." I hung up before she responded.

****

Weightless, I drifted on my back. Letting the water cradle me, quiet and cool, my body finally remembered how to let go. Overhead, the ceiling fan turned in slow, deliberate circles. Steady and unbothered, like it had nothing to prove, nothing to want.

I didn't know if she would actually show, but I'd hoped to be cloaked in her caramel-coated embrace by now. The ache of not knowing settled in the hollow of my chest.

I let myself sink to the bottom. My trunks clung to me like skin, soaked, stubborn, holding on the way I hadn't let myself admit I was.

I held my breath as long as I comfortably could, then I surfaced through the silence.

Water trickled slowly down my face, my vision obscured by the liquid veil.

When I blinked the blur away, there she was. Standing at the far edge of the pool, barefoot.

Silent.

Watching me.

Like she'd been there all along. "You actually came." The words slipped through with a smile as I took in her black two-piece.

"You really didn't leave room for no," she said as she sat down at the pool's edge. I swam to her like I was trying to reach shore after nearly drowning in everything I couldn't say.

She curled her knees in close, her toes teasing ripples across the surface.

"I'm just glad you're here," my elbows resting on the pool's edge as I looked up into the portrait of beauty framed before me. "Now I know you know it's okay to get wet." I added, narrowing my eyes with a wicked smile.

I pushed myself off of the wall and swam backwards to the center, keeping my eyes on her the entire time. "You getting in, or you gonna stay there looking like something I dreamed up?" I called out to her before she slipped in and glided through the water like it parted just for her.

My chest tightened around the rhythm of my heart. I hadn't dreamed of this moment. She was right here in the flesh. She stood in front of me now. The water rippled around her perfect frame like a seductive dance. Droplets clung to her skin like they weren't ready to let go.

The words were on the tip of my tongue, a potential turning point for us. I choked on the words. So instead, I just said, "You look good."

There was something heavy inside her eyes. Something familiar I just couldn't quite put a name to.

She wasn't just standing here for me. Ayana had showed up for herself as well.

At first, she said nothing. Neither did I. Yet, in the stillness, a weight seemed to lift from my shoulders. Having her here, bare and brave, felt liberating. It was like a breath of fresh air; I had been holding out for.

With a delicate touch, her palms grazed my arms before her hands clasped around my neck, their pressure gentle yet sure. Her eyes, pools of dark emotion, delved into mine, searching for something hidden there. Then she whispered, "I missed you."

I anchored my hands at her waist, pressing my lips to her forehead before returning the sentiment.

"I missed you, too."

11

TEMPERED BY FLAME
(Yah-Yah)

I stood in front of the mirror in his luxurious bathroom, blow-drying my locs, swallowed up in his oversized t-shirt. This was not supposed to be the way I started my day.

I pulled my hair up in a bun, grabbed my phone and headed into the hallway to find Eli. I could smell something wonderful coming from the kitchen.

A professional chef greeted me when I stepped into the kitchen; of course, he had a chef. Why would I expect Eli to be the one cooking? I shook my head but returned the greeting before journeying on to find Eli.

He sat in the center of the sofa, sweatpants hanging low on his hips, the television's muted glow reflecting in his eyes, flipping through channels as if it were just another morning, not the aftermath of something sacred. The rise and fall of his bare chest was hypnotic; I couldn't tear my eyes away from the steady beat.

"You've got a whole chef in there whipping up a five-star breakfast with sizzling bacon and fluffy pancakes, while you're out here glued to the cartoons?" With a pointed look, I asked, my arms folded tightly.

He looked up, a smirk playing on his lips as he saw what was in front of him. "It's not cartoons; it's anime." He said through clenched teeth, almost insulted. "And you were sleeping so peacefully, I couldn't bear to risk ruining your rest with burned eggs and a kitchen filled with smoke."

I paused, taking in the scene before finding a spot to sit. I just watched him, the silence between us heavy with unspoken words, unsure if I wanted another moment of his quiet presence or the answer to the question burning in my throat.

"So," I murmured, "is this something you do often?"

"No, Ayana," he smiled, "they don't normally stay the night."

Playfully punching his chest, I added, "Well, I'm pleased to be your breakfast guest." I was reaching in to kiss him when the jarring sensation of my cell phone vibrating in my right hand stopped me in my tracks.

Today 8:30 AM

Sky:
Ok, kitty cat, puuuuuuuuuuur!

Me:
We need to figure out how to give this
Soul Steppin' thing a doorbell.

Sky:
Knock Knock. Now, ma'am, get it in and
bring your ass to the shop, cause
Titi wanna rap to you.

Me:
I'm about to eat breakfast. Stall for me a bit!

My aunt's urgency was going to have to wait for an urgency of my own. I climbed on top of him, tossing the remote and my phone both aside. He didn't resist as I leaned down and whispered in his ear, "Oh, you don't cook, but do you serve?"

"Only if you're starving."

His hands found my face, thumbs dragging gently across my skin. When he pulled me in, my thoughts short-circuited.

"I could eat," I said, although hunger didn't feel like the right word anymore.

He gripped my hips, then-

"Breakfast is served, sir," the chef's voice came from the kitchen like

a perfectly timed punchline.

We froze.

I dropped my head to his chest, and we both burst out laughing.

"You just *had* to be fancy and have a fucking chef." I climbed off of him, not showing how much I really didn't want to.

"Next time, you can just cook," he said, glaring up at me.

"Next Time?" I said, shaking my head as I turned to walk away.

"I like my steak medium rare."

I looked over my shoulder. "Boy, you can't even cook."

He shrugged. "Doesn't mean I won't learn, especially if I get you as the reward."

I rolled my eyes. "You are so full of yourself."

He grinned. "That makes two of us."

We both took our seats at the table. Everything received beautiful plating, a feast for the eyes and stomach, showing meticulous attention to detail. A rich aroma of sizzling steak, seasoned with herbs and spices, mingled with the buttery scent of fried eggs, filling the air. Letting the taste linger, I inquired, "Do you offer this to everyone?"

"No," he said without looking up. "Just the ones I want to stay."

"Eli," I paused, "I need to get to my shop. My aunt needs to speak to me. And I have clients. So after we eat, I'll call my Uber. "

"What do I need to do yo get you to come right back?"

I didn't answer right away. I dragged my fork across my plate, searching for the right thing to say. His eyes were still focused on me.

"Eli, what exactly are you asking?"

He took a sip of his coffee, taking a moment to reflect.

"I'm asking what I have to do for us to stop pretending this doesn't mean something."

He set his cup down, steady now.

"I'm asking if there's a version of this where you come right back."

His words knocked the wind completely out of my chest. I don't know what I expected him to say, but it sure as hell wasn't that.

I'm not sure I've ever been with someone as direct as he was. Part of me wanted to say yes without even thinking. The other part of me was still learning how to trust.

"Eli, I have to go home later, and you can't send your driver every time you want me. You don't get to snap your fingers and have me fall inline," I didn't mean for it to sound like a rejection; I just didn't want to lose control. I had put my life together piece by piece, and no one, love interest or not, was going to make it crumble. "Eli, I'm not saying no. I'm saying there has to be some give and take."

He pushed away from the table, stood, turned, and left the room. Leaving me speechless. I was about to go gather my belongings when he re-entered.

"Cancel your ride, cause I know you already scheduled it."

"Eli, come on, I have things to-"

"I want you to be able to come whenever you want to." He placed a key fob in front of me. "No driver."

"I am not taking your car, plus that convertible is way too flashy for me to be driving in Eli. That's not my speed."

He chuckled, "In no world would you be getting my convertible? That's a Jeep Wrangler, and it's all yours."

I stared at the fob. "A Jeep?"

"Yours." He added, "Yours when you want to come here. It's even yours when you don't."

I hesitated, fingers brushing it but not picking it up. "This doesn't mean I'm yours, Eli."

"I know," he said. "But I want it to mean you have a way to choose."

Before I could say anything, my phone buzzed

> Today 8:45 AM
> Sky:
> That kitty must be a damn hellcat, bitch!
>
> Sky:
> Oh shit, Knock Knock!

I let out a light laugh, then pocketed the key fob.

"Show me this chariot."

****

To avoid my aunt's questions about my new vehicle, I planned to arrive at the shop at the perfect time, but my plan backfired. When I pulled up to the shop and parked, both Titi and Skylar were standing in front of the salon. My fear hadn't even allowed me to notice what they were making a fuss about in front of the shop. I eased out of the driver's side and casually tried to pass by.

"Oh, I know you fucking lyin'." Stopped dead in my tracks by Titi's piercing signature drawl. "When we completely forget our damn manners? I ain't sleep with your ass last night, now did I?" Titi continued.

"Yikes, now that would have been freaky," Sky added, not exactly helping.

"Sky, shut up!" I fired.

"What in the hell is this monstrosity, Ayana?"

"It's just a vehicle?" Dear God, why would I say it like that and *not* expect a storm to follow?

"Oh! Just a vehicle! Now what was I thinking?" she started. "I guess you, as a spectator, was not enough for him, huh? That flashy grand marshal didn't even have to wrangle you onto a float. You just marched right in." The storm raged on. "He has himself a willing krewe participant. Leading the charge in a shiny new...*vehicle*." She spat the words out like they turned her stomach. "Doing only God himself knows what this morning." I glimpsed the view behind her, and my heart stopped.

"Meanwhile, we over here cleaning up all this shit something or someone left behind."

The reason they were both outside was when I pulled up.

My sidewalk container garden, once a source of pride, was now a depressing display of dead plants; even the soil looked parched and cracked.

My mind drifted to the last time I was here. Eli and I moved recklessly in the alley, the dim light that wrapped around us reflecting off the cool brick as my back rammed against it.

Skylar slid over quietly, leaned in close.

"We gonna tell her you rode the float? Or..."

"Skylar, I swear to God. That is not helping."

I yanked open the salon door.

"And I didn't even sleep with him last night," I snapped over my shoulder, storming inside and sinking onto my stool at the bar.

They both allowed me a moment of silence.

I was trying my best to get adjusted to my new space in this world, but everything was moving at lightning speed. I was in *my* shop on a day we are normally closed, and I got cursed out like a little kid for reasons I'm sure I just didn't understand.

Titi walked past the bar without a word and disappeared down the back hallway.

There was only one door down there, and I'd never had the key. I always thought the basement belonged to another business.

Then I heard it.

The sharp click of a deadbolt unlocking.

Of course I did.

"So another secret?" I muttered as Skylar trailed after her.

Titi's voice echoed up the stairs.

"Just come the hell on!"

The air changed the moment I stepped off the last stair.

It felt cool still and sterile.

The lights above us were motion activated, lighting our way with every step.

Glass-lined shelves stretched from floor to ceiling all around me. They were climate controlled and cradled strange objects pulsing behind the glass.

Further in, I saw bubbling flasks, glowing beakers, and strange objects suspended in fluid.

I stopped where Skylar was sitting behind a computer, typing away.

"What is this place?" I asked, my voice low. She just chuckled.

"Just come over here and sit with me for a bit. She will be calm soon, I'm sure. Let me give you the lay of the land." Skylar pushed back from the desk.

"Like I said the other day, for most of your life, your powers have been what we call unvoiced. That means it was just in your bloodline, but not active." I held on to her every word.

"We had no way of knowing when you would gain full control of your powers. Because you are both Protector and Empath, this place would have been impossible for you to enter without you feeling like you were going insane." She said so matter-of-factly.

"When I dropped out of Nova Tech-"

"After only being there a year, mind you," I cut her off.

Not a smile or a single joke followed. She just continued without her normal antics.

"When I dropped out of Nova Tech and came back home, because I missed home. Almost immediately, I got to work on developing a series of mechanisms that would protect you in this environment and allow you the best opportunity to learn. What you see now is what I eventually developed alongside Titi. I call it Spell-Tech." This was new to me, seeing her so calm, reserved. And I loved it.

"So it was a whole damn Hogwarts up under my hairdryers this whole got-damn time?" At that, we both laughed.

"Hogwarts came first, fool." She added. "This was your father's vault before we converted it into our lab. And when you took an interest in opening a shop, Titi acquired the property above it."

"What was it before-" I almost jumped out of my skin. "What the hell is that?!" I screamed as a slender, shiny robot with a red bandana tied around its head and knotted at the front was approaching us with a tray like a server.

It handed Skylar the tray, which held a chilled bottle of wine and two glasses.

As it extended the tray, its movements suddenly became jerky. The robot's head twitched, and a metallic grinding sound came from its joints.

And just when I thought I'd seen it all... the robot spoke. "Th-th-this won't fix-fix-fix it," it stuttered as its voice modulator glitched, "but it c-c-could help her face—" The robot froze mid-sentence, lights flickering across its control panel.

"Dammit, not again," Skylar muttered, quickly grabbing the wine before the tray tilted. She reached behind the robot's neck and pressed something.

The robot whirred back to life. "—it." It finished its sentence as if nothing had happened.

Skylar smiled apologetically. "Thanks my G," she said with a nod. "Yanni, this is my lab mate, The Underground Brain of Our Tools...or, you know, TUBOT."

TUBOT.

Of course.

Even in her genius bag, Sky was still a damn goofball.

"Still working out some bugs," she added, tapping the robot's shoulder. "His neural net is advanced, but the power distribution system is... temperamental."

She poured us both a glass as TUBOT turned and walked away, one leg dragging slightly behind the other.

"I think he saw you needed a lil help taking all of this in." She chuckled.

I gulped.

"So that thing is waiting tables; that's what it was designed for, huh? To be frank, I have no idea what he's supposed to be doing." Titi had returned from her cooling-off period.

"He's supposed to be assisting with relic analysis," Skylar sighed, "but right now he mostly brings wine and shorts out at the worst possible moments."

She didn't miss a beat. "Alright, Sky. First things first, do we have a record of that quilt you said y'all saw? You know, the one you found while you both were in Tha' Barrows, blatantly defying me?" She said it so casually, we almost missed the scolding tucked tight inside her tone.

"And define...defy." Skylar shot back, stalling.

"Lord have mercy." Titi continued, "so you were both so smitten that it just slipped your mind to check? At all?"

"Sky," my eyes narrowed. "Smitten?" I snapped.

"She's just speculating," Skylar said. Almost too quickly. Her eyes were already back on the screen.

"Speculating my ass," Titi chuckled from her gut. "She's just over it already."

"Okay, I think I may have it right here. Just give me a second," Skylar said while typing rapidly. "You'll just have to confirm before I update the record."

Titi leaned in toward the screen, scanning the file.

"Okay, Ayana. Tell me if this is what you think you saw."

I leaned into the screen slowly.

The first thing I saw said **The Ember Veil.**

It felt familiar.

My chest tightened, and I didn't even know why yet.

I scanned the description. Protective textile. Fire-Weavers of the Sahel. Emotional signature: grief, endurance, survivor's guilt.

Then, I saw the image.

It was a long, tattered cloth. A bold red with a deep ember glow stitched through the folds. It looked worn, but not fragile.

I didn't remember touching it. But I knew what it smelled like.

My mouth went dry.

"Yeah..." I said, barely above a whisper. "That's it."

Titi's gaze softened just a tad as she let out a labored breath.

"Okay. Now we can update the new location in the database."

"What does it all mean?" I asked, still trying to process what I'd just read.

"It's a relic," Titi said. "Woven to protect the user from fire. But it doesn't work for just anybody. It only responds to people marked by it."

She turned to me. "By fire, and by loss."

"It glows when activated," Sky added. "Smells faintly of smoke. Holds memory, not just magic."

She paused. "Also… it responded to you. That's when you slipped through."

"And we have a database for every relic?" I asked slowly, catching on.

"For generations, our bloodline kept a handwritten record of the relics we protected and the ones we came into contact with," Titi said, motioning toward a glass case behind the desk.

Inside was a tattered leather journal that looked older than time.

"That's where I come in," Skylar said. "I wasn't about to let her keep writing by hand when we had technology at our fingertips."

She gestured toward the screen. "The database is called RIAN. The Relic Identification and Ancestral Network. Now everything in that book is located inside here."

"And… the Veil?" I asked.

"In the 1800s, our family used to protect it," Titi said. "But the record lost track of it in the mid-20th century."

"Now, somehow, it's in Bibi's possession," Sky chimed in.

Titi's eyes snapped to hers. "Eli and Ali's grandmother." Skylar said.

Titi tried to hide her skepticism but lost that battle fast.

"Titi, I know what you're thinking. But it's really not like that. Neither of them are Echo Hunters," Skylar said. "The old woman had some weird shit going on, sure…but everyone read pure."

"It's something about that other one though," Titi muttered. "Ali is a complete angel… the performance at Griot's Groove…I'm positive he's not just talented; there was magic in his message."

"That's just not how genetics works, though. Eli can't be the exact opposite of his brother magically," Skylar argued.

Titi turned to me. "Ayana. What about the charm he wore? I have an inkling, but what about you? Do you feel something from it?"

I didn't even have to close my eyes. The weight of that night came rushing back tenfold. His heat pressing into my skin… and then, the memory of when I touched it.

My stomach dropped. I went pale.

Skylar and I locked eyes, both of us suddenly on the edge of tears.

I couldn't find the words. All I could do was nod.

Titi held my stare. "That's confirmation enough." She paused, taking a moment to gather her thoughts.

"When I saw him at the festival, I sensed a relic I'm charged to protect. But I know exactly where that relic is located."

She paused. "I know it's damaged, though."

"It's here?" Skylar asked.

"Yes."

"Then let's look."

Titi didn't move. She looked uneasy, her eyes drifting to me.

"Ayana will be fine," Skylar said, trying to reassure her. "The tech won't let her get overwhelmed here."

We followed Titi through the lab, past rows of glass cases, until she stopped in front of one. I couldn't see what was inside at first. The tinted glass concealed everything.

Titi waved her hand in front of the case, and glowing symbols bloomed across the surface. Runes or a language I couldn't read.

She squinted, leaning in. The symbols shifted as if responding to her presence.

"This is the one," she said, pressing her palm to the center of the glass.

The tint vanished.

I stepped closer for a better look.

Inside was a charred black bone, brittle and crumbling under the weight of years. Age stained its surface; a deep red cord bound it tightly. The cord stood out against the smooth, dark bone. Glowing etchings pulsed down its length, the light slow and rhythmic like a heartbeat.

Then the pulse quickened.

A silent flame rose from the top, tall and unwavering.

The room felt hotter.

I stepped back quickly. Skylar pressed her palm to the glass, causing the tint to return.

My pulse slowed instantly.

Relieved.

"Whoa" was all I could say.

Titi placed a comforting palm on my cheek. "Originally, this relic was in your father's family possession. This is the bone torch of Nakia," she said, her voice calm. "Nakia was a feared and respected high priestess. As legend has it, Nakia called down a divine fire to cleanse a corrupted temple overtaken by greed and betrayal. Unfortunately, she died in that fire." She said somberly.

I didn't move. I wasn't even sure I could.

"Her bone remained. It didn't burn and never decayed," Titi continued. "Her loyal followers wrapped it in red silk, marked it with symbols, and made it into…a weapon."

She glanced towards the case. "It reveals the truth, a stark and undeniable reality. Summons spirits. Burns what needs to be burned. But it's not gentle. The torch doesn't care if a lie protected the innocent or if the truth will hurt. It brings it all to the surface." She let that settle in the silence before adding softly, "That's what I felt when I met him, Ayana."

"That's chilling...but I didn't observe any of it missing. It can't be both here and with him at the same time."

"I can't put my finger on it," Titi said slowly, "but something's...off. Somehow it knows him." Clearly unsettled, Titi pulled a pouch from her bosom, clutching it tight with her right hand.

"She'll be fine," Sky said. "Let's just give her space to do her thing. Come check out the greenhouse; we can grab some things for your garden."

I followed her, but the question kept pressing.

"So... you and Ali," I asked, trying to sound casual as we reached the greenhouse.

She glanced over her shoulder. "What about him?"

I stopped walking. "Sky, come on. Did you fuck Ali?" I asked, plain and loud.

"Did I..." Her voice trailed off as she opened the greenhouse door. She chuckled, closing it behind us.

"What do you even wanna know that for, Yanni?"

"So... yes?"

"Like a fucking porn-star."

"Where?"

"His grandmother's restaurant."

"Oh my god... you are impossible. I swear, you might be rubbing off on me a little though."

"Yeah, right,girl. I can't imagine you doing shit wild," she said as she started choosing fresh plants to transfer to the sidewalk garden.

"We kinda did it here."

Sky froze. "Pardon?"

"I slept with Eli here."

"In the greenhouse?"

"Bitch, this is my first time in the damn greenhouse."

"Ayana, then where?" She wasn't asking like she didn't know. She was asking like she hoped I was wrong.

"In the alley. The last time I closed the shop."

Skylar stopped. Her skin turned pale.

"The alley?" She leaned in closer. "Ayana, has he ever been inside the shop?"

"Uh, no?"

"What about your crib?"

"Not yet. I usually go to his place. Why?"

The study was just a little way down the hall. The air smelled like sweet smoke, maybe incense. I followed Skylar inside.

Bookshelves stretched from floor to ceiling, packed with old paper and stranger things.

She went straight to a shelf and pulled a black book with a worn binding.

The spine read: Classifications and Behaviors of Supernatural Beings in Urban Environments.

She moved to the table deeper in the room and flipped it open, her eyes scanning fast.

I sank into the chaise lounge at the center of the room, trying to ignore the weight of this feeling. In her silence.

Suddenly, she slammed the book shut.

"I need to go see Titi."

****

I could barely keep up with Skylar as she flew down the hall to a small, dark room.

When we stepped inside, the air felt thick.

Titi was gathering a pile of bones, shells, and smaller objects. She placed them in her pouch and set it gently on her altar with a silent prayer.

"He is a chosen vessel," she said, her voice low. "But someone made that choice for him. Selfishly. He carries Nakia's legacy, though he has no idea. And in carrying that legacy, if he's not careful, the fire could reignite the full wrath of her passion."

She took a long, drawn-out breath.

Whatever magic had once kept him safe was now fading, leaving him vulnerable, and only one person knows the truth. The one who knows keeps it hidden. Even from him."

She paused, her words slow.

"That necklace he wears? Is a pendant of betrayal. It doesn't just hold his power; it's shaped him. Into what, I'm not exactly sure. But it's in that necklace."

Skylar stepped forward, her voice barely above a whisper.

"It still doesn't explain why you sense the other relic," she said. She held out the tattered book, the page folded at her notes. "But I think I know what it could be."

Titi grabbed the book, listening closely now.

"He's never stepped foot inside the shop. Never been inside Ayana's home, either. Maybe because he can't. Not without a cost. Every moment they've shared has been at his place."

"Those eyes," Titi said. "That energy. Emotional feeding?"

"How's his body so damn perfect?" asked Skylar

"Gold's Gym, chile, now focus," Titi warned.

"The dead flowers," Skylar added. "Ayana said they were fine the night before when she was with him… outside. That means they died overnight. You saw them. They weren't just dry; they were parched, like brittle leaves in the fall. Their color washed out, like faded denim. It was as if an unseen force had swept through, draining the very essence of life from them, leaving them empty shells."

"Some spirits don't take. They feed. Slowly. Quietly. They just charm you first," Titi said.

She turned her gaze toward the altar.

"He sucked the life out of the flowers. Fed on their life force. If I'm right, it's not just relic magic shaping him. It's something older. Something that feeds." She paused, choosing her words carefully. "Some spirits don't need blood. They drink what you feel. Love. Grief. Pleasure. They linger where the energy is thick, and feed without taking a single thing you can see."

Her attention returned to the altar, something from the bone casting still tugging at her.

"It's not just the magic," she murmured. "There's something older than he knows. And it… feeds."

"Obayifo?" Skylar whispered.

"Obayifo," Titi agreed.

Obayifo.

Somehow, my spirit not only understood. I think it had been waiting for the confirmation.

Now that it had come, it held me in a chokehold.

"So… what are we thinking here? She can't go back there with him. Can she?" Skylar asked, looking at Titi.

"Why wouldn't I?" I said, trying to keep my voice steady. "You both literally said Even he doesn't know. Even if he is a predator, does that automatically make me his prey?"

Sky rolled her eyes. "Not a demon dick fiend, Yah."

"I'm serious. You just dropped a name on me like a curse, and now what? I walk away from him? Hide? After you, of all people, encouraged me to fuck with him in the first place? That's not how this ends, Skylar."

"I'm just saying... he doesn't have to mean harm for harm to happen. I've already seen this whole fucking movie before, drama queen," Skylar hissed.

"Girl, you fucked his brother in his grandmother's restaurant bathroom, and I'm the one that's extreme?" I shot back.

"Okay..." Titi started calmly. "I don't see the need for any of that, girls. Let's not attack each other." She paused, gathering her thoughts. "I say... you do go back, Ayana."

"Are you serious?" Skylar snapped.

"Now your slick mouth is finna write a check your hot ass can't cash," Titi said, eyes sharp. "This would not be the opportune occasion to play with me."

"Yes, ma'am," Skylar muttered, her tone quieter now, eyes lowered.

"Now, as I was saying, before I was so audaciously interrupted," Titi continued. "Ayana, you go. But you don't just go as the woman who loves him. Now that you know who he might be... you need to know who you are."

"Not just dangerously in love," Sky added, "but a magical field agent?"

"So I'm just supposed to go back and... what? Spy on him?" I asked, my voice catching. "Pretend everything's normal while secretly investigating him?"

I stood up, pacing the small room. "This is crazy. Yesterday I was falling for him. Today you're telling me he's some kind of... emotional vampire? And I'm supposed to be what? Your undercover agent?"

"Ayana..." Titi began.

"No," I cut her off. "You don't get it. When I'm with him, I feel... alive. Complete. How am I supposed to look him in the eyes and pretend I don't know what you're telling me? How am I supposed to touch him and not wonder if he's just... feeding on me?"

My eyes stung with tears. "And what if you're wrong? What if he's not what you think he is?"

"That's exactly why you need to go back." Titi said softly. "To find the truth. For both of you."

Skylar stepped closer. "Yanni, if I thought he was pure evil, I wouldn't let you within a mile of him. But this is... complicated. He might not even know what he is."

I sank back down into my seat, the weight of their words settling over me.

"I need time to think," I whispered.

"We don't have—" Skylar started.

"Give her a minute," Titi interrupted, shooting Sky a warning glance.

I closed my eyes, trying to sort through the storm in my mind. The memories of his touch, his smile... against the dead plants, the strange feeling when I touched his necklace.

"If I do this," I said finally, looking up at them both, "it's not just for you. It's for him too. If someone's using him, manipulating him... he deserves to know."

Titi nodded slowly. "That's exactly right, baby. This isn't just about protecting you. It might be about saving him too."

That, more than anything, was what convinced me.

Titi continued, "If you're going back in, I will not be letting you go empty-handed."

"Real talk," Sky said, already moving. "We need a crash course on your power. Be right back."

Titi turned to me, voice low but urgent. "Now I've gotta be real with you. It normally takes years for someone to learn full control of their gift. And we don't have that kind of time."

She was already moving, grabbing a cloth from the altar. "We're going to set you up with some spell-tech to help along the way. First things first, I'm putting a sigil on this handkerchief. Keep it close. That way, if you slip without knowing, you can always find your way back without getting lost."

She began drawing fast, her hands precise.

"Umm..." Skylar reappeared in the doorway, one brow raised. "I was thinking something a little more permanent."

A faint buzz filled the room.

She lifted her right hand, a tattoo gun humming softly in her grip.

12

FIRE AND FURY

(Eli)

Alone at a corner booth in my grandmother's place, I sat tracing the rim of my whiskey glass with my forefinger. I didn't want to be here.

The smell of steamed shellfish hung in the air. For once, I wasn't quite hungry. The plate in front of me was completely untouched. I'd been dodging this place for days.

Dodging her.

She quietly slipped into the booth across from me, slightly startling me when I looked up.

"Now you look way too low for someone on top of everything," she said, holding a small grin.

I pushed the glass a little farther away. My eyes stayed focused on the table.

"Not hungry?" She asked, gesturing to the untouched plate.

I shrugged.

"What has you off-kilter?" She questioned, glaring at me through those chilling, pale eyes.

"I'm just exhausted."

"Oh? Well, I guess missing product is enough to exhaust anyone, isn't it?"

I lifted my eyes slowly. Her grin didn't move, but her stare was deeper.

"Yes, we resolved that issue; Roderick was relieved of his prior duties."

"Yet he sits right outside in the parked truck?"

"He's just my driver now."

"A mistake like that and one still can afford the lap of luxury, hmm," the nail of her pointer tapping my whiskey glass.

"Oh, so now I threw him a party just cause I didn't blow out his candles?" I asked in a huff.

He ought to be relaxing in the dirt beneath the warehouse, but you're correct, son; it's been taken care of. "

I slouched deeper into the booth.

"You have the weight of way too much on you, my dear. Let me relieve you of some of that pressure." Her hand closed around my necklace, pulling it towards her; my heart slowed, and breathing became difficult.

I couldn't move

She leaned in closer. "The problem you seem to have is you think you get to walk away from your power unscathed."

The pressure in my chest thickened as my vision faded.

"You don't get to choose what you are." She continued, "You only get to choose whether you survive it."

Just when I thought I was a goner, she released me, knowing she had made her point.

The pendant dropped against my chest like a grenade. I gasped.

"Now," she said, smiling like none of that had just happened, "eat."

I emptied my glass instead.

She let the silence stretch a little, then tilted her head.

"You still seeing that girl? The Broussard?"

"Ayana?" I asked, surprised by the shift. "Yeah. Why?"

"No reason... just be sure that she stays in her lane. Girls like her bring light where it may not belong, is all."

"She's not a problem..."

"Just be careful where you place your affections."

"I didn't ask to be the way I am... at least I should be able to have a life away from all of this." I dragged my fork across my plate.

"Hmm," she looked over at the quilt on the wall, "and at what cost?"

"At whatever cost." I replied.

Her gaze was still on the wall. "You and I witnessed the same thing here in this room, Eli, but I guess only one of our eyes was open."

"What are you talking about now?" I asked, dropping the fork in front of me and pushing the plate further away now.

"I do not think she even understands, but she sees. It's in her bloodline. She comes from a line of protectors...and she just shows up on your doorstep?"

"Bibi, Ayana is not up for discussion." I barked.

"There is the control I've been waiting for.."

"That's enough." I stood fuming.

"Is it now? Cause I thought we were just getting started." She hissed.

"You've made your point, Bibi."

"You think you can run away from what you are? Your hunger is your inheritance. Yet you look at it like a curse." She held her mouth in a slight smirk, like she knew this battle was hers. "Just be ready for what might happen when she see's exactly who you are.

13

THE FLAME WITHIN

(Yah-Yah)

I stood in front of the full-body mirror, shirtless, in a black bralette. My flesh, still freshly tender. The tattooed compass on my sternum glowed below my skin's surface.

Strangely enough, it felt so normal, almost like it had always been there.

I could feel a slight pull from the compass when my direction changed.

All of my senses now felt supercharged.

Sky stood a few steps behind me, her watchful eye keeping close tabs on my emotions as her combat boots frantically tapped into space behind me.

This moment marked a new beginning. I could physically feel the shift.

"Now, once we start this, there is no stopping Yanni. Are you sure you are ready for this?" Sky asked.

"Well, it's no unknowing what I know now either," I replied.

The tapping of her boot ceased instantly as she offered a silent nod of approval.

Titi approached slowly, observing my expression. "I know you'll be properly dressed and well-behaved when you see him, of course, but surely you've thought about justifying Sky's artwork, haven't you?"

I nod, wondering exactly how that part would work.

"You'll find out all too quickly. Most people can't even see what they don't understand." She waved a hand in front of me, and the tattoo vanished from my reflection. I peered through wide eyes in disbelief.

"Look outside of your reflection," she directed my gaze down.

There, the tattoo glowed like it had never left.

"So, it's hidden?" I asked.

"No, not hidden," Titi added. "You're not hiding it, you're carrying it; that's a big damn difference."

"Okayyyy!" Skylar sang from behind me. "It ain't invisible, baby. It's just yours." She smiled softly, grazing my shoulder. "Now that you know what it looks like... let's show you what it does." Skylar motioned for be to move into the open space of the room.

"We start simple," Titi said. "With what you are. Not what you can do."

Sky held my hand in hers, both of us barefoot, facing each other. I stood tall, mirroring her.

"Close your eyes," she directed. "Now...feel."

First, I focused on my feet.

Heavy.

Overcome by gravity.

I could feel myself dropping through the floor below me.

Suddenly, I felt myself falling - not physically, but like my consciousness was dropping through the floor. My heart raced, panic rising.

"Yanni! Come back!" Sky's voice sounded distant, muffled.

I gasped, eyes flying open, my body swaying dangerously. Sky caught me before I hit the ground.

"That's what we're trying to prevent," Titi said calmly. "You just slipped without control."

My legs felt like jelly. "I didn't mean to.... I just...."

"We know," Sky said. "Let's try again. This time, don't surrender to it. Command it."

I closed my eyes once more, steadying my breath.

"No...don't let it happen to you. Claim it," Sky corrected me.

Instantly I was back on the ground... no. I *was* the ground. I felt like I had never actually *stood* before. Not like this.

Now I noticed my breath. In. Out.

It was linked to my stance. Every part of me connected. And with every turn, the compass followed... no. I was following the compass.

"Now, as you move, keep the moment you are in right now," Skylar instructed. "This is your new normal. Fall from it, and the compass will remind you."

My heart and thoughts were running the same race, and I couldn't tell who was winning.

Skylar guided me to a mat on the floor. I sank down, legs folding beneath me, breath still trying to catch up.

"Sit in it. Feel what presence feels like on ya," Titi's voice wrapped around me, gentle and steady, almost like a lullaby.

"Now let's see if it holds," Skylar said as she moved away behind me.

A sharp crash split the quiet.

Loud.

Metallic.

It rattled through the room.

Jolted my body.

My newfound peace slipped straight through my fingers.

My heart scrambled.

But before anyone said a word, before I even thought to ground myself, the compass pulled.

Not forcefully.

Not harshly. Just enough to guide.

And somehow, I was back.

Breath steady. Cool, calm, and collected.

The shift didn't belong to anyone else. It was all mine. "Now that's what the fuck I'm talking about!" Skylar came back, running a celebratory lap around me.

"Okay chérie, that's quite enough." Titi said, entering back into the room. Upon her approach, she placed a tarnished locket in my palm. It turned ice in my grip. My fist trembled.

What I held in my hand. Once had love and laughter surrounding it…then there was silence. Like I was holding a last goodbye.

Instantly my heart felt three times its weight. My eyes filled with tears. I pulled my knees towards my chest and silently wept.

"Yanni, this is not *your* pain." Sky stooped down, reminding me where I was. "Understand how to observe without absorbing." She stroked my cheek with the back of her hand. Honor that moment, just don't drown in it." I understood her, but I wasn't ready to let it go.

"Master the art of witnessing what others can't," Titi said, taking the locket from my hand.

Without a word, she pressed something new into my palm. A small brass key.

It turned hot the second it touched my skin.

The heat pulsed through me, slow and steady, until it settled deep in my lap.

My breath caught.

This wasn't grief. It wasn't pain either.

It was... want.

Need.

My hips moved on their own, chasing the object of my desire.

But then the pull from within reminded me to return to the center. My breath steadied.

"Good," Titi said, gently taking the key. "It wasn't perfect, but you found your way. That's the lesson. Desire can't be followed blindly. Remember where you need to be, even when you want to lose control."

"I can't even lie. That one had me fighting for my life!" I said as we shared a laugh.

"You resisted, but you still got pulled in first," Titi added more seriously. "That's what we need to work on - preventing the initial pull."

"But I found my way back," I said, still proud of that much.

"You did," Sky acknowledged. "But out there in the real world, even a moment of lost control can be dangerous. Especially with him."

I nodded, sobered by the reminder. This wasn't just training. This was survival.

"You're doing superbly, Yanni. Most people have years to get to this point. You've had literal hours. That's a testament to your power," Sky said, with a hint of concern in her voice.

"So why am I different?" I asked genuinely confused.

Titi and Sky exchanged a look.

"The trauma you experienced as a child," Titi said finally. "Sometimes... great pain creates channels in the soul. Pathways that others have to work years to build."

"Your powers were activated by extreme circumstances," Sky added. "Your connection with Eli, his energy... it's like someone threw you in the deep end. You're learning to swim because you have to."

"But that doesn't mean it's safe," Titi cautioned. "Fast learning doesn't equal mastery. It just means you're surviving."

Sky moved to the far side of the room and spread several objects across the table.

"Now, we have to… kick it up a notch," she added, her tone more serious as she motioned me forward.

"Umm, okay," I muttered, stepping closer.

As I approached, the surrounding air shifted, reminding me of a held breath.

A small rectangle of paper caught my eye. Folded. Worn. Just visible in the faded ink were two words: Admit One.

The second I read them, the soles of my feet burned. A chill cut through me.

Then, the surrounding room disappeared.

I was at the rear of a small community theater.

The air was thick with dust and something I couldn't explain. Something much older than me.

The house was full. I stood in the center aisle, observing everything around me.

No one in the audience even turned to look at me. No one seemed to notice me. All the focus was on the stage ahead.

She stood center stage, commanding the room.

An older woman with bright eyes and perfect posture spoke her lines with playful ease..

The audience was spellbound.

I didn't budge.

And then I heard it.

Heaven flowed from her lips.

The notes, however, concealed something deeper. A whisper threaded with sorrow..

The melody cut through the air and curled around my rib cage, constricting the air in my lungs.

My heart tightened.

She sang each word with the lingering relish of a last taste.

The notes clung to her like they weren't yet ready to say goodbye.

Raw emotion filled the atmosphere

Then…after the last note. She collapsed.

The audience burst into applause.

A rapturous standing ovation.

Yet, she didn't rise.

They applauded.

Loudly.

She lay there lifeless.

They roared. Blind to the death right in front of them.

The applause swallowed the silence that should've been reserved for her.

Without another thought, I leaped onto the stage and frantically attempted CPR, but my hands passed through her chest, hitting the ground beneath her with a thud.

Then the audience, stage, and her, all slipped out of my sight like sand spilling through an hourglass.

With a blink.

I was back. The ticket still in my hand.

The room spun as I tried to steady my stance. I could still feel the melody wrapped tight around my torso. My palms throbbed. Raw from pounding the ground, trying to save her.

"Whoa…" was all I could bring myself to say. "I don't think I'll ever get used to that," bracing myself on the table.

I was exhausted.

Sky stood silent, eyes locked on mine, taking a moment to really see where I was.

"You saw what happened to her," she said, voice low and steady. "She kept pretending she was okay when she wasn't. Smiling through it. Singing through it. Performing."

She took a breath. "The compass only works if you use it. That's what it's for. When the world pulls at you. When you get lost inside." Sky paused. "Lose sight of yourself too long, Yah… you don't just fade. You vanish."

She placed the ticket and remaining objects into the aluminum briefcase and latched it shut.

"As an empath, your body tells you everything you need to know. Start *using* it instead of *letting* it happen to you." Sky's voice sharpened. "Before you slip, your feet burn at the bottom. That's not punishment; that's prep. And when you come shooting back into your body, land with the same amount of control. Same energy both ways. Mastering that makes it Soul Steppin'. Walk into it."

Her eyes narrowed. "It's a visit." She leaned in closer. "Stop acting like it's an abduction."

"Now that… is a whole word," Titi said. "You preaching up in here today, Skylar."

I let out a breath. "It's just… there's so much to learn. So much to remember. When will I actually be ready?"

Titi smiled, full and soft. "Baby, you were born ready." She placed both hands on my shoulders, steady and sure. "Now you just have to trust what's already inside you."

She held my gaze, then added, "One more thing to know: as a Protector, you take on the power of the relic you interact with. It's part of your DNA."

"But it's not a damn bar trick, Yanni," Sky chimed in.

Titi laughed low in her throat, not letting go of my shoulders.

"She's right," she said. "The power ain't for showing off. It's for when the moment calls for it."

Skylar tossed me a freezing bottle of water. "Hydrate. You look like you just sprinted through hell. And I know damn well you ain't going to that man's house to watch TV." Her grin was wicked.

Titi looked up slowly. "Go on then... let love teach you both something." Her eyes narrowed. "Just don't forget your compass is with you if you lose your way."

As the silence settled, my phone buzzed, pulling me back from my thoughts.

8:30 PM

ELI:
"To wait an hour
is long
If Love be just beyond
To wait Eternity
is short
If Love rewards the end."

ME:
I didn't have you pegged
as a Dickinson fan.

ELI:
She was onto something.
Also...I'm on to you, Ayana.

ME:
Is that right?

ELI:
Yup, you like the chase.

* * * *

ME:
Okay, so you have no clue at all.

ELI:
If you say so.

ME:
Then, are you familiar with her piece
about patience?

ELI:
"Patience
is the Smile's exertion
Through the quivering."
But I resonate more with the
Brooklyn poet that said
"I got no patience, and I hate waiting."

ME:
Cute

ELI:
Did it work?

I didn't respond. I just smiled and started to gather my belongings.
He could wait a little longer.

I said my goodbyes and headed towards the stairwell. But before
my foot hit the first stair, Skylar gently grabbed my wrist. She pressed
a small pouch into my palm as I turned to face her.

"I want you to have this," she spoke in a low tone. "It's from when I
first learned my way."

I opened the pouch, revealing a tiny handmade marble, painted
with faint swirls. It felt warm in my grasp.

"If you just need to stay in a moment, hold on to it. With this, you
won't be able to slip; it anchors you in the present." She hugged me
tight, almost like she didn't want to let me go. "You've learned enough
to start, but not enough to be safe. Not yet."

Her eyes were serious. "If anything feels wrong - if you slip and
can't control it, if your emotions overwhelm you - use the marble.
Don't try to be a hero."

I nodded, understanding the weight of what I was undertaking. "I know my limits."

"No," she corrected me, "you don't. That's the point. You've had one day of training for something that takes years to master. You've done amazingly, but…"

"I get it," I said. "I'm still a beginner."

"Yanni, if you need me, I'm already there, okay?"

I nodded. "I know."

14

BENEATH THE FLICKER
(ELI)

The silence in my apartment didn't bother me until tonight.
Tonight, nothing moved. Not the air, not the shadows.
Just me.
Waiting.
I poured myself a whiskey, neat, and sank into the middle of my sofa, before lifting my glass and taking a sip. The whiskey, smooth and comforting, slid down my throat with a warm, welcoming sensation.

I told myself I wasn't waiting for her. Still, I kept glancing toward the hallway, expecting to hear her footsteps.

I got up and walked over to my vinyl display case.

My collection spanned across several genres, a patchwork of decades and moods. Coltrane, Davis, Wynton & Branford Marsalis, Marcus Miller, Chick Corea, Joshua Redman, Eric B, and Rakim, 2Pac, Lauren Hill, The Notorious B.I.G. and so much more. Each record is a phrase in the story I'm still telling.

Slowly, I ran my fingers across the spines, admiring the musical treasures in my palm.

I settled on Glasper's Black Radio.

I dropped the needle and let Erykah curl through the atmosphere, soft and smoky.

Somehow even absent, Ayana was right here, in between each note.

Slipping through the downbeat and dancing slowly to the melody.

****

Still not ready to sit with the quiet, I crossed back to the record case. My fingers grazed the familiar titles until I found a burgundy spine.

"Oh yeah. This is the one."

The needle dropped.

After the hit of the first snare, a slow drone from a custom keyboard patch slid across the beat. Lazy rhythm moving off center. The bass held it down, steady and full.

Then that voice.

Raspy.

Smooth.

I moved through the apartment, slowly dancing with nothing but the air and my memory. Two-stepping between notes. Half a glass in one hand.

By the time the chorus came in, I was already singing with him.

That raspy texture layered over a sultry melody.

Chords rooted in gospel as they flirted with a certain sin.

So smooth

So right.

Hanging on to the last note, I was in my world when…

"Wait, you sing?"

Her voice came from the hallway behind me.

I turned, startled but not surprised.

There she was. Leaning against the doorframe. I didn't answer right away. She didn't need me to.

Her eyes scanned the room slowly.

"You got company?" She asked softly. She almost convinced me she was serious.

"Well, she is finally here," I shrugged.

Just like that, the room not only wasn't empty anymore, but the space invited her with open arms.

She stepped into the room, still scanning the space. When she reached me, she took the glass from my grip. She didn't ask, just took it like it was already hers. Taking a sip, looking deep into my eyes. Searching.

"Was I invited to the party?" She asked, still picking at it.

I nodded. "The guest of honor."

She smiled, then ran her finger down the center of my chest.

"So… what song plays next?" her eyes still penetrating mine effortlessly.

I smiled back. "Depends," I said, walking towards the record player. "You want some trouble, or you want something tender?"

"Tender," she sighed, plopping down on the sofa, slipping off her shoes and curling her legs beneath her.

I flipped through until I found exactly what I was looking for.

The moment the needle hit, the energy shifted.

Al's voice floated in smooth like velvet.

Did you say I've got a lot to learn?

She looked up with a seductive grin.

"Okay," she said, a hint of a smile playing on her lips, "you understood the assignment." Rising gracefully, she met me in the room's center, her footsteps silent on the plush carpet. With a soft sigh, her arms reached up and clasped around my neck, her touch gentle but firm.

I clasped my hands at her waist.

We let the music take us somewhere familiar, together.

"You know, I worked an entire shift and then some today, yet you wanted me to come here instead of, I don't know, maybe meeting me at my place?" She said, her head cocked to the side. She removed her right hand from my neck and placed it deep in her pocket. "I mean, I know I don't have a fancy chef, but I have a dope little spot in Royal Hills." She continued.

We still swayed slowly to the song. Her eyes rested comfortably in mine.

I had held her this way before, but this felt different. She felt… grounded.

With her right hand still in her pocket, she traced my jawline with her left. Still looking.

"You're the one who said you prefer trouble, Ayana." I replied with a slight grin, my hands roaming curiously across her backside.

"Sometimes…trouble is where it all starts, Eli. Maybe trouble is exactly where it ends." She asked.

I smiled, but something about this moment was pushing my grin to tighten. The way she held my gaze. So steady, so sure. She removed her hand from her pocket. Holding onto a small object. A marble.

Before I knew it, she was gripping my necklace with her other hand. Her gaze was still steady, but now she appeared to be seeing somewhere beyond me.

"Ayana," I whispered, my voice catching in my throat. Her eyes nestled in mine once more.

"Eli?" she said, her voice tinged with concern. "What are we doing?" Her grip was still on the necklace.

"Umm, Dancing," I bounced back, looking down at the marble she held. Still swaying side to side.

"You know, I used to think I was just imagining it. But the more I'm around you, the less that works." She placed the marble back in her pocket. "If *we* are building something. I think we could benefit from putting it all on the table." Her grip was still on the necklace.

"There may not be enough space on that table. I'm… not…" the words, caught in my throat. The charm glowed in her grip. Now she was looking directly at it.

"I'm more than who I seem to be on the surface, Eli." She started. "I…can see." She said, releasing her grip on the charm. "I'm from a long line of…Protectors. And no, I haven't always known what that meant. But it is who I am. And I want you in my life."

The charm dimmed on my chest now, but I could still feel the heat from her traveling inside me. "You want *me* in *your* life?" I said almost to myself.

"I'm not asking for every answer, Eli. Just saying, don't leave me in the dark. I'm already holding the match." She said.

"I should tell you what I really am," my voice trembling slightly.

"I think… I already know," she said hesitantly.

"This isn't something I chose for myself." The weight of my heart increased by the moment.

"I know that too."

"And I want to be in your life too," I held her tighter. Now her arms were back around me, her hands clasped at the base of my neck. She leaned against my chest, relaxing into me as if this moment took a load off of her shoulders.

With a final hiss, the record came to an abrupt end, silence filling the room. Just the soft click of the arm looping in place was left in the crackling silence between us.

Neither of us moved.

15

SMOKE SIGNALS

(Yah-Yah)

I woke up in his arms. My head nestled in the space where his chest met his shoulder.

Our bodies spilling into each other. A caramel confluence.

I studied the rise and fall of his chest, wading in the ripples of his relaxation.

Carefully, I slid out of his embrace, looking back at what had become my solitude. Trying not to disrupt the quiet escape of his slumber.

There's still a part of me that flinches at peace like this, like it's too good to be true. I had let go, but part of me couldn't help but wonder how long this would last.

It's been three months since the first night we shared our truths. Since then, I've been right here with him.

We didn't talk about forever. But every night, we returned to each other as if it were a promise.

I barely knew him, yet I felt like I'd been waiting for him my entire life. This made no logical sense; we'd only just met. But logic didn't seem to apply when it came to Eli. There was something pulling us together that defied explanation, something that made hours feel like years and touched parts of me I didn't know existed.

I was about to reach for my robe when I felt a pull at my wrist from

114

behind me. Then fingers interlaced with mine.

"Don't go." A demand disguised as a request. "Not yet." His raspy tone spoke to my body before my mind could process it. His eyes not even open, he grasped at what he knew to be familiar.

Before I knew it, I was turning back to him, letting his hand pull me into the heat of his chest.

Letting his mouth touch me tenderly as he rolled on top of me, making me a prisoner to his embrace.

One kiss led easily to the next, his lips sketching me from memory.

My hips invited him to erect monuments as he sculpted a masterpiece of pleasure inside me.

I didn't hold back as I fell back into this sacred space we'd been building together for months.

Quiet.

Warm.

And full of him.

****

Wrapped in a black silk robe and the scent of him, I moved barefoot through the quiet. The warmth of safety clung to me, like I belonged here.

Once I reached the kitchen, I fell into what had become my Sunday morning routine. Reaching for a mug left out for me on the counter, I started the water in the fancy kettle hand-painted with dazzling neon colored floral art.

It was clearly out of place in the matte black kitchen. He had purchased it just for me a few weeks prior. Said that maybe now the space needed a pop of color. Maybe *I* was the pop of color *he* needed as well.

The scent of dried lavender rose with the steam, mingling with honey, filling the room, easy, like Sunday morning. I cupped the warm mug in both hands and stood there for a while, letting the silence settle into me.

He always slept in after late nights at the club, the rhythm of his life so different from the beat of mine. But little by little we were finding our groove.

I took my cup to the living area and sank into the sofa wrapping a black fur throw around me.

This room had grown on me. The lavish interior a direct contrast to the boho flair in my place.

And no, I hadn't moved out of my home... not completely. I still liked having my own space. Though Skylar was there more than I was now.

Claiming my spare room after an unfortunate quarrel with Mark, her better half. She hadn't said she was staying for good, but her plants had found their way into my window seal and a collection of her original art found its way to my welcoming walls.

Turns out two empaths may not be the perfect match after all. Skylar was honest about her affair with Ali and Mark completely lost it. His once gentle shower of love had swiftly become a vicious hurricane, then a chilling blizzard.

I took another sip from my cup, reflecting on the love lost. I reached to grab my cellphone that buzzed on the coffee table before me.

Speak of my angel...

7:30AM
SKY:
Hey punk!

ME:
Hey punk!

SKY:
Well, look who jumped off the soul pole long enough to answer a text from her long-lost friend!!!

ME:
Lmao, he's sleep fool.

SKY:
Oh ok. Now you're on your Suzy Homemaker shit?

ME:
I'm relaxing with my morning tea.

SKY:
Ok tea. Well, your aloe is good as dead. And I'm bout to eat the last mango, okay?

* * *

ME:
Just disrespectful! I will pick some up today.

SKY:
Bring Prosecco!

I smiled at the screen, shaking my head. She was chaos and comfort in equal measure.

I set the phone down and stood, stretching a bit before I padded toward the kitchen. My empty mug cradled in one hand. I washed my mug and wiped down the counter.

I started a lot of coffee for Eli, knowing he would be up soon.

Then I headed back to the living room, where I took a moment to fluff the throw pillows and fold the blanket I'd just been wrapped in. His scent clung to the fabric. Musk and a hint of bergamot from the oil he liked to wear. That scent always softened me.

I returned an abandoned stack of records back to their case on the wall. At the record player, I smiled. Remembering the night he played Al, the night I bared it all.

This man and his music.

I straightened more records out of place on the shelf. Once everything was in order, I made my way down the hall to the bar area.

From the looks of it, he made a pit-stop here before coming to bed this morning. His shirt thrown about the barstools back. His wallet sat in the middle of the bar top beside his keys.

A lone whiskey glass and decanter clicked as I returned each back to their rightful places on the shelf behind the bar.

His cologne still lingered in the room. I stood there a moment, taking him in.

I grabbed his shirt, bringing it to my face without even noticing what I was doing. The scent calmed something in me.

I gathered the rest of his things: wallet, keys. I shook my head. He always leaves a trail.

This was starting to feel normal. I moved through his space with a kind of quiet ease, like I had always belonged here.

I stepped into the hallway and headed toward the walk-in closet just outside the bedroom.

I pushed the door open with my shoulder, balancing everything in my hands, and stepped inside. My foot caught on something, and I stumbled forward, barely catching myself.

His shoes.

Clearly, he was in a space when he arrived home early this morning. His belongings were carelessly discarded in his path.

I looked down at the misplaced shoes, annoyed.

As I bent down to grab them and place them where they belonged, something about one of them felt… off. When I picked up the pair, something shifted inside one.

I flipped it over.

Something small slipped out and hit the carpet with a soft thud. It rolled a few inches, then stopped.

A bright pink hair bead. The kind that dangled at the end of little girls' braids back in grade school.

It wasn't exactly alarming… just strange.

I reached for it.

The moment my fingers closed around it, the air snapped.

Heat surged up through the soles of my feet like the floor had caught fire.

I steadied myself, breath tight, grounding in the feeling.

The closet blurred, then disappeared.

Metal walls pressed close around me, cold and smooth beneath my fingertips.

A faint hum whispered through the air, coming from somewhere just beyond one of the panels. A generator maybe, humming to keep this place alive.

I blinked, letting my eyes adjust to the dim light.

Someone had taken old shipping containers and turned them into a series of makeshift rooms. Stacked and sealed, with no windows. But there was electricity inside and even a bathroom with running water.

I stepped slowly further inside.

The floor felt solid beneath me, but the air shifted with each movement.

I caught the low murmur of voices somewhere ahead.

Careful and slow, I followed the sound.

Staying close to the wall, I stepped lightly. The hallway opened into a larger room lit by low light.

Three girls sat on a daybed at the far end. A TV glowed in the corner, playing cartoons. Blankets tucked tight around them. Their eyes were wide but silent.

I stayed in the shadowed edge of the room, my heart pounding.

Then I saw him.

My love.

No. It couldn't be.

He stood in the corner, just far enough not to touch them. Watching. Quiet. Still.

Not cruel, but not kind either.

And the girls, they feared him.

Then his face shifted. It was him, but not him at all.

I wanted to reach out, to touch one of their hands. Help them somehow. Offer something.

Anything to soften the fear in their eyes, to lighten their burden.

But before I could get close, something shifted.

The air tightened around me. I couldn't catch my breath.

I sensed fear, yes, but something more.

Something older.

This was bigger than him.

Looking closer, he wasn't himself at all.

What stood before me was an older version, harder, darker, something that had taken over.

It wasn't just him anymore.

My heart was pounding, but I caught myself, grounding back to the present. I had to get out of this moment before it swallowed me whole.

I steadied my breath, focused my thoughts, and willed myself to let go.

With a sudden rush, the metal walls faded, replaced by the familiar quiet of Eli's closet and a familiar voice.

"Hey baby." I dropped the bead in front of me.

There he was, standing in front of me. His chest bare, silk pajama shorts clung to him like a caress.

At first, I didn't say anything. I continued placing his items where they belonged. Then I stepped to him. I touched his face gently. I traced his chest. I let my fingers run through his locks. Just trying to show myself this was the him I knew and had grown to love.

His skin was warm, real. Nothing like the cold shadow of the other him still burned into my mind.

"Dont get something started you aren't prepared to finish right here, right now, girl," he frowned, his body responding to my touch.

Of course, I wanted him right here, right now. Then the chill on the girls' faces caused me to simmer down.

"I started your coffee. What you want for breakfast?" I asked, slipping past him and heading toward the kitchen.

The heat of him followed.

In the kitchen, I grabbed my phone for a rushed text.

* * *

8:30AM
Me:
SOS

SKY:
Meet me at the lab in 30

I sat my phone on its face and rushed to look normal.

When Eli finally came into the room, he stepped up behind me at the island. Brushed against me, his body telling on him before he said a word.

"Babe, sit down so I can feed you before I have to get out of here. Now, Jesus." I nodded toward the counter. "Your coffee is over there waiting."

He didn't move right away. Just stood there behind me, breathing heavy down my neck.

"E!" I was almost irritated now.

He chuckled and sat at the outer side of the counter where his coffee was waiting. Picking up the mug, his golden eyes gazed from behind the rim. Following my every move. From the fridge to the stove, back to the counter.

His voice, low and lazy, "Why you always trying to boss me around?"

I chuckled too. His charm was unforgiving.

I prepared his breakfast in silence under his stare. His steak perfectly seared, beside hash browns and scrambled eggs.

"You know, you could have kept the fancy chef," I said as I placed the plate in front of him.

"Not a chance," he replied, grabbing a handful of my ass in the process.

I pulled away and sat across the island on a stool opposite him.

"I have a few thinks to handle today, and I need to meet my aunt at her office after I check on my place. Do you need anything while I'm out?"

He glanced up from his meal. Shrugged.

"Just save some trouble for daddy when you get home."

*****

* * *

"I found something at his place," I blurted the moment my foot hit the bottom stair.

Skylar peered over her screen, eyes narrowing. "Found…what exactly?"

A voice rose from deeper in the lab. "Well, is that a tornado or my niece, storming up in like manners ain't never met her?"

"Hi, Titi," I said as I stepped fully into the room. "Sorry…" I dropped into the chair beside Skylar. "How are you?"

"Well, I was perfectly fine before you came barging in here, messing up everybody's peace but yours."

Skylar leaned back in her chair, arms folded. "So? What happened? What did you find?"

"A hair bead," I said.

"A…hair bead?" Skylar repeated.

"Ayana, don't piss me off today," Titi snapped.

"Listen, I know what it sounds like, but it wasn't a regular bead."

"Go on," Skylar said, eyes locked on me now.

"The kind you'd see dangling off little girls' braids. Like Serena Williams back in the day."

Titi threw her hands up. "Ayana, you've got seven seconds to make this make sense or get outta this goddamn lab with your nonsense!"

"Yanni, a hair decoration is not—"

"I stepped when I touched it!" I cut her off.

The room around me felt like it was closing in. My stomach was in knots as my heart thumped in my chest. I felt like I was right back at the apartment again.

Titi looked to the ceiling. "Lord, give me patience if not discernment." Then back at me. "Why the hell wouldn't you start with that?"

"I'm sorry. It just kind of happened. I was cleaning up some of his stuff, and it fell out of his shoe."

"Cleaning up?" Sky echoed, looking disgusted.

"When I went to pick it up, I stepped. But I was strong. Controlled."

"So you didn't shift?" Titi asked.

"Not at all."

"Well, go on, baby, tell us what you saw," Titi said, leaning in.

"I saw metal walls. Cold to the touch. I realized I was inside a converted shipping container. Someone had made it livable…divided into rooms. There was power. Lights. Even a bathroom. It wasn't fancy, but it worked."

"Ayana," Skylar said, sharper now. "What else?"

I hesitated. "Three girls. Wrapped in blankets on a bed. A cartoon was playing in the corner. They weren't crying, but... they looked scared."

Skylar's face tightened. Titi said nothing, just watched me.

"They were the missing girls. I know it. From the news reports."

I swallowed. "And then I saw him. Eli. He was just standing there, watching them. Not hurting them, not saying anything. But they feared him."

I paused. My voice dropped. "It was him... but it wasn't. His face, shifted. Something else was there. It was almost like it was wearing him."

Skylar pushed back her chair. "What are you even saying?"

Titi held up a hand. "Let her finish."

"I'm saying I'm sure it was him, but he turned into something or someone else." I repeated.

Skylar narrowed her eyes. "Turned into what?"

"This may be the answer to where his relic comes from, or who cursed him." Titi said as she rose to her feet.

"Wait," Skylar said, voice sharp. "Are you saying the relic *made* him change? Like...*physically*?"

I shrugged. "It looked like him but older...colder. "

Titi's eyes flicked to Skylar. "An echo can trap more than memory. Almost like her sight was showing her the blueprint."

Skylar crossed her arms. "Blueprint for what though? Some other version of him?"

Titi nodded slowly. "To the curse itself, what it wants him to be."

Skylar frowned. "So she saw what he will be?"

"Not exactly," Titi said, moving around the lab, her eyes scanning the shelves. She paused briefly, then left us standing there as she headed toward her altar room.

Skylar shifted uneasily. "Maybe we should give her a minute."

"Maybe." I agreed.

Skylar and I sat in silence as we waited for what we knew was coming.

I'd seen Titi do this many times before. She called it her "work." Once in her altar room, she'd lay out her conjure cloth and draw the pouch from its resting place. Inside, chicken bones, knucklebones, and bits of shells clinked softly together, worn smooth from many years of falling on each other to tell someone else's truth.

She didn't rush.

She never did.

By now she was already speaking to the ones who came before her, asking for sight, clarity, and truth.

Then she'd toss the bones.

And wait for them to speak.

After a while, Skylar and I peeked through the doorway.

"How nice of you two to finally come join me," Titi said from deep inside the room. "Sit. I already asked; now we wait for the answer."

We eased in, and she didn't look up. Her eyes stayed fixed on the spread of bones and shells, fingers tracing slow circles in the cloth.

She pointed to a cluster near the center. "That's bloodline. Wrapped tight. This isn't a coincidence."

Skylar squinted. "Bloodline? You mean his?"

Titi nodded once. "Blood that's still with him. Carried. Close." She pressed her palm flat against her chest.

Skylar frowned. "Wait. You mean… the necklace?"

Titi didn't blink. "Not a haunting. A hold."

Skylar's voice dropped. "The crescent moon. That's ivory, right?"

"Bone," Titi said softly.

Skylar flinched. "Bone? Whose?"

Titi looked at us both. "The necklace he wears was forged from the Bone Torch of Nakia."

Skylar stared at her. "That's why you felt it. But you're saying it's not a fragment of the torch?"

"I'm saying the Torch made it," Titi said. "That crescent is all that's left of the Obayifo that was burned alive in Nakia's rage." Her voice dropped much lower. Her fingers stroked the cloth beneath her. She took a deep, slow breath. "It was once Eli's grandfather."

The air went still around us, shock maybe. Titi didn't look up as the silence explained better than she could. My mind flashed to the image of the crescent on his bare chest. It was always there, like it were a part of him.

Skylar's eyes, shooting me a sideways glance. "Eli is wearing his dead granddaddy around his neck?" She inquired through her disgust.

My mouth went dry. I could still feel it in my hand, the way it pulsed, like a second heartbeat. Heavy. Warm. Alive!

I swallowed hard. "His grandmother said…it was his… legacy."

"Wait, does he *know*?" Skylar asked in a rush. "Does he know he's wearing a bone fragment?"

Remembering the way he looked when I asked him about the necklace at his grandmother's restaurant. "I don't think he knows." I exhaled deeply. "At all."

"So he just got that shit on him all raw, no protection, no clue." Skylar's eyes narrowed. "Doing its bidding too?"

"That's not legacy…it's straight up slavery." I interrupted. "She knew, didn't she? His grandmother. She knew what it was all along, and she gave it to him, anyway."

Titi's eyes lowered, her breath slowed, and she nodded slowly. "She knew." Her words came crashing in. "It's possible she thought she was protecting him. At first, anyway. Keeping her family's power close." Titi lowered herself into the chair beside her. "But legacy without knowledge…ain't a legacy at all. Is it? And him carrying that curse blindly could be dangerous for him and everyone around him." Titi stared into the space in front of her. "We have to save him from it… before it finishes what it started."

"And Ali" I asked.

"I told you from day one that boy is special." Her tone softened. "I'm positive both are born protectors. They just never learned the way," she continued. "And I think Ali is among the rarest of our breed."

"No," Skylar shot a skeptical look. "You think? Like, for real?"

"I believe Ali is a Resonant. If Eli can destroy the world and anything directly around him…then Ali can save the world and everything in it. He can save the world with just his voice and his music alone. A fail-safe hidden in his DNA."

"Nature over nurture." I added. "She destroyed one, and the other can make it right."

Skylar stood staring into the space before her.

"I'm telling his brother." Skylar said to no one in particular.

I knew it wasn't a question. Her decision was already made, and you could not change the mind of a determined Skylar.

"Okay, well," I searched her face for a soft spot. "Maybe just don't yell it at him with your clothes *off* this time?"

The corners of her mouth hesitated, then stretched into a wicked grin.

"Oh, baby, you got me fucked up for real. I ain't never been the one yelling. Upside down or right side up. Hear?"

Titi shook her head. "I should know by now to expect crass from you two, even in the middle of a crisis." She rolled her eyes, but a laugh had already crept through. She and I let it carry us for a moment, just long enough to feel something like normal, while Skylar gathered her things to head out.

"Ok goof troop, Ima roll now. Gotta go see a man about his monster." Skylar gripped her bag, pausing for a moment in the doorway like she was bracing herself. "Don't forget to ground yourself, alright?"

She gave me one last look, half teasing, half warning. "You're still sleeping with the enemy. If you even *sleep* at all."

With that, she was gone.

And she was right. I hadn't once considered not going back to him.

And for the life of me, I don't know how I got here.

******

The moonlit sky hung low as I eased through the streets toward Eli's. Though I'd been there many times, the destination felt foreign. Music thumped through the speakers, but it barely registered; my head was just in the clouds. With the windows down, the night air rushed in, but it couldn't cool the slow burn building in my chest.

I pulled into my parking spot and just sat there, hands on the wheel, gazing in front of me at nothing in particular. I just wasn't ready to move.

Then, the thought of his warm arms around me was enough to move me from where I had been planted. I slid out of the Jeep and shut the door behind me.

The elevator ride was much slower than usual, no rush, no anticipation.

Just going down...slow.

When the door opened, the hall was dark. Still. From here, I could already see the trail of his clothing leading to the bedroom.

No way, not tonight. I let them stay exactly where they were.

When I stepped inside, he was in bed, the glow of the massive wall-mounted TV playing over him. Skin the color of warm caramel caught the light, stretched over muscle, sprawled across black silk sheets. When he finally recognized I was standing in the doorway, those golden eyes spilled all over me. I told myself to remember what I knew. Instead, I drowned in what I wanted. Needed.

My fingers toyed with the hem of my shirt slowly, almost unsure. I drew it over my head. Each step toward him felt heavier, yet I kept moving, leaving a trail of fabric behind me. His gaze followed every inch I revealed, and the space between us thickened until we were breathing the same air.

I slipped into the bed beside him, his hands grazing over every inch of me.

A sculptor at work.

I was his masterpiece.

His kisses spoke in a language only my body remembered.

He asked. I answered.

Our bodies pressed together, his skin melting into mine, wrapped in a heated embrace.

But somewhere inside that warmth, I felt something colder.

A faint draft slipped under a closed door.

Then it grew, filling my chest, crawling up my spine, spilling into my gut.

"Eli," I whispered, pushing gently at his chest. "Stop."

He stilled.

His gaze hovered over my face, searching, calculating.

Then the gold in his eyes went dark.

Cold.

Cold enough to make me forget we had ever been warm.

16

CROSSFIRE

(Eli)

I knew something had shifted the moment I woke. I should have said something then, before the day breathed life into it.

Instead, I played coy.

Puffed out my chest.

Loved her with every part of me that knew how.

Maybe if I had shown her everything first, she wouldn't have been so confused.

She wouldn't have been afraid.

I knew Ayana's power. She told me she was a Protector, and I'd watched her own everything she was becoming. But the moment I saw her in the closet, I knew.

She didn't just have the power of a Protector. She traveled too.

Whatever my baby had seen shook her to her core. I should've talked to her then. Should've promised her we'd be okay.

Instead, I let her leave.

She had been gone all day.

All day, I worried she wouldn't come back.

Then I saw her in the doorframe.

Beckoned her close.

Searched for a safe place to hide inside her.

She was tailor made for me.

More than desire; I was trying to hold on to her, scared of what might pull us apart. I tried to push that feeling away. Then she pressed her right hand on my chest, pushing me backward.

I could have simply stopped.

We could have spoken about her fears.

But I didn't.

Instead, I let the silence taunt me.

Threatened to taint my forever.

I let my anger boil, burning hot beneath my skin, blinding me to everything but the sting of being misunderstood.

I stood and gave in to my rage.

Screaming like I wasn't just making her moan for me.

The words shot out too much, too fast. I didn't give a damn if they broke us.

Those words replayed in my head now… in her absence.

"Eli, you don't have to be this way. Can't you just try to change… for me?" she begged through tears.

I yelled, "What now? You're the authority on all things magical?"

Her voice shook. "I'm saying you don't have to carry all this alone. You don't have to be the curse."

I laughed bitterly. "What fucking curse? You think it's that easy? That I can just choose not to be who I am?"

"It's not about choosing, Eli. I'm asking you to fight…with me. Not against me."

"Fight? What if fighting means losing you? What if I lose myself?"

She pushed back, desperate. "And what if we get a chance at something normal? For fuck's sake, Eli, you can't even come into my home. Can't set foot in my shop. I'd rather lose you if it means I get the real you."

I looked away, the weight of her words hitting me hard. "Maybe I'm already gone."

I knew I'd pushed her too far. She turned to leave, and I grabbed her wrist, begging her to stay.

She pulled away as if I were nothing. I called out to her.

At the door, she looked back and said, "Why would I want to stay with a motherfucker who won't even save his own soul?"

With that, she was gone.

It was only last night, but it felt like weeks without her.

Every shadow in the room seemed to stretch longer without her in it.

I'd let the best thing that ever happened to me walk away without a fight.

Now, every text sat on read.

Every call rang into nothing.

I sat in the living room, staring into nothing.

The buzz of my phone made me jump.

For a split second I let myself believe it was her, ready to talk.

One glance at the screen killed that hope. No such luck.

A video call.

My grandmother's scowl filled the screen.

"Were we meeting today? I know old age hasn't taken my memory just yet."

"Bibi, no, it hasn't," I admitted. "I just haven't left yet. I'll be there soon though."

"And Ali is nowhere to be found either. Not like him at all," she added, narrowing her eyes like she was already piecing together a theory I didn't want to hear.

"Oh? Not your golden boy finally a little tarnished?" I snickered.

"Brunch…" she hissed, dragging the word out. I already knew she'd follow it up with something sharp enough to kill whatever appetite I had left. "Bibi, I'm getting dressed now. Be there in a flash."

"Bring one of those fancy bottles to make up for your tardy arrival, yes?" Her tone carried the weight of command, wrapped in the sharp edge of accusation.

Not that I had forgotten our standing brunch date. I just didn't care. I wanted to be wherever Ayana was. Nowhere else.

I pulled myself off the sofa and stepped into the shower. The warm water felt grounding, a small sense of normalcy in a day that had none.

I pulled perfectly tailored black slacks over my designer boxer briefs, tucked in a slim-fit black button-up, and fastened a black leather belt at my waist. I pulled on my Oxfords and headed to my bar to grab a bottle for the old woman. Woodford Reserve, the Baccarat edition. This should be good enough.

It was time to go.

On my way out, I caught a glimpse of myself in the mirror. Cloaked in black from head to toe, with the crescent moon on my chest caught the light. I touched it, the cold metal a reminder of the line neither Ayana nor I could cross. Even as she comprehended every secret, I was too stubborn to embrace her optimism.

******

The car ride far east was quiet. Only the hum of the engine kept me company, steady and low, while my thoughts swarmed about. My brother hadn't answered my texts or calls, and he wasn't at his apartment when I stopped by to see if he wanted to ride together.

He wasn't the type to go completely ghost. Not unless something was wrong. The more I thought about it, the longer and lonelier this drive felt. Between Ayana's icy silence and my brother's sudden absence, those I cherished seemed miles away. I was stuck driving towards an unwanted place, with only my questions to ride shotgun.

I pulled up at Bibi's place. Ali's car was nowhere in sight. The restaurant, though, thrived, full of people eager to eat at one of Nevermore's finest tables. As I moved through the busy dining area, the aroma of food wafted through the air, and I greeted the staff on my way to the back. The heavy basement door loomed as I stood before it, dreading the journey down.

My descent down the steps was almost painful. I took reluctant, heavy steps. The dim blue light from the aquarium walls on each side of me rippled across my steps, pulling me further down until the current carried me into the mouth of my disdain.

In the basement, Bibi stood behind the bar, calm.

Unbothered.

This was her domain.

She slid a step to the side as I approached. I set the bottle down and sat.

"Well, well. I guess the prodigal son returns," she said, her dark grin dripping with sarcasm as she stood behind the bar. "Now what sorrow held you back? Sulking in your solitude instead of tending to your family, hmm?"

"Bibi," I shook my head slowly, "It's nothing." She cracked open the bottle and poured a portion of the spirit into a glass she placed before me.

"Is being behind on profit considered nothing now?" She shot back, holding me in the grip of that pale stare.

I didn't have a moment to respond before a sound like an explosion rattled the room behind me. Ali stormed down the steps and burst through the door. His bloodshot eyes, sharp and exhausted and burning, locked onto a face I knew too well, now twisted with raw rage.

"What's wrong, baby bro?" My voice cracked against the tension, uncertain, unsteady. I had never seen him like this.

But he didn't look at me. His gaze, like an arrow, flew past me and landed directly on our grandmother.

"You wanna tell him? Or should I?" he spat out. The venom was potent enough to make me want to drop to my knees. "Matter of fact, did you ever plan on telling him? Telling us?!"

His chest heaved as if he were holding back a scream, fists clenching and unclenching at his sides. The atmosphere was cracking from the weight of his fury, anger ripping out of him as if he had been searching for this moment to come tearing free.

"What is this, child?" She said, calm, unmoved. Untouched by the poison he pronounced.

"I stood caught in the middle, peering between the brother who had always been the better half of me and the grandmother who raised me as her own. Their words tore through me, syllables embedding in places I could never reach.

I wasn't sure what I was missing as Ali paced back and forth. For a moment, everything went still. Then, "Tell him!" he roared, voice breaking the air open.

I jumped, liquid, now airborne, rushing from my glass. My sight locked on him with wide eyes, breath caught in my throat. When he looked at me, I saw the pain holding him hostage. His eyes locked on mine and then flooded. I watched his rage collapse into compassion.

His tears spoke before he said a word. Something had completely undone him.

"Eli," he cried, voice breaking. "She did this to you." The words struck like a blade, sharp and merciless. "She made you. But this wasn't supposed to be who you are."

"Made... me? What?" I was completely confused.

"Ali, that's enough of this. No doubt that harlot friend of his, that Jezebel, has gotten into your head," Bibi said, her tone clipped and cold.

Ali snapped toward her, voice shaking with rage. "Don't you dare put this on anyone else! This is of your doing. You know damn well it's you."

"What's going on, bro?" I asked, voice breaking. My eyes flicked between them. "Bibi?" I wanted answers.

She drew in a slow breath, her eyes never leaving Ali. "Don't let his foolishness confuse you, child. He speaks from a place of weakness, not truth. He's never had the power that you do. "

"You selfish fuckin'.." He started, but I grabbed his arm, pushing him out of her path.

"Bro, watch your mouth. The fuck is wrong with you, Ali? That's your grandmother." I tried to reason with him, but the words only made his chest heave harder.

He ripped his arm from my grip. "Exactly, Eli. She's our grandma. And she was supposed to protect us. And she doomed you instead."

"Ok buddy, what did you take?" I placed my hand on his cheek. "It's okay."

He pushed my hand away, slow, almost tender. His voice barely carried. "She… your necklace. That's the relic that makes you Obayifo."

"No, Ali." My jaw tightened. "It's the only thing that keeps it calm."

"A lie," he snapped, his eyes cutting to her. "Just a wicked lie she fed you so you'd serve her. Tell me, Grandmother, did you save us from a fire you started yourself?"

"I lost everything in that fire. I lost my son, my home. Your grandfather built that empire. I had to watch it burn to a crisp with my only child still inside."

"My grandfather was a criminal and an Obayifo! A fate you forced on my brother."

"The heir apparent was Eli."

"What the fuck are you even talking about, Bibi? We are born protectors. That you know, cause it's a gift we received from your blood. Yet you taught us nothing about our lineage. Taught us nothing about our actual power. This empire here, you built on weaponizing the very thing you were born to protect." He laughed. "I'm sorry, not you. Cause you would never have been able to do it alone. So you made my brother a fucking monster!"

"Ali.." She reached for his shoulder, but he jerked backwards the moment she connected.

His voice was a desperate cry as he spat, "Get away from me!" His face was a perfect picture of disgust, "You know what's crazy…I bet if you had given him a choice, he would have done it anyway, for you!"

Again, our eyes connected. I didn't know what to feel, so I reached out. His grip was tight, trembling, a mirror of every fear I thought I had buried. I held the back of his head as he wept into my shoulder. After what felt like an eternity, he pushed away, steady enough to stand on his own. I watched my reflection, my twin, walk out without a word.

She didn't deny it.

My grandmother said nothing at all.

Bibi's silence filled the space he left, a tide heavier than anything she had ever spoken.

17

SCORCHING TRUTH
(Yah-Yah)

The moment I reached the Jeep, the sky opened up in a violent downpour. My grip quivered on the steering wheel. The streets were slick under the tires, and the thick night pressed against my windshield like a heavy burden. I could still feel the heat of his anger tiptoeing across my skin.

The city lights burned bright as the memory of his screams. I drove away from his rage, irritated at every stoplight that halted my retreat.

I was safe now and headed to the safest place I knew.

Once I reached the front door and stepped through the threshold, two sets of concerned eyes landed directly on me.

Skylar searched my face for answers to questions not yet spoken. She stood from her seated position and forged forward until my cheeks rested inside her palms. "Yanni?" her voice, a psalm.

With salvation within her grasp; I sank into her grip.

I tried to push down the only words that could explain the horror of my night, but the feelings were impossible to ignore.

Skylar was now in tears, a ball of raw emotions, sensing every stanza written for my heartbreak.

Ali, beside us now, met our breakdown with concern. His eyes darted from me to Skylar, trying to read the words I couldn't say.

"Ayana?" His voice was a gentle brush, silk on a coarse surface.

I flinched at the sound, too close to Eli's tone, a jolt of fire I wasn't ready to face. Skylar's fingers moved through my locs, root to tip, slow and steady, grounding me in the moment.

I wanted to explain, wanted to spill the horrors of the night, but shame stuck to my tongue. The words clung to the back of my throat. I let the silence hang, leaning into Skylar's touch, letting Ali's eyes plead while I stayed locked inside myself.

Skylar guided me further into the room. She took her seat back on the sofa, and I settled between her legs, resting on a zafu pillow at her feet. She continued raking through my hair and rubbing from my neck to my shoulders; my mind kept drifting back to him. Each memory of his anger felt like fire on my skin, though Skylar's touch was a cool counter to it. Ali stooped down beside me, though he stayed quiet, sensing the weight of what was unfolding.

I showed her his eyes, the way they went from worshipping me to targeting me as the source of his aggression. I showed her how he went from pressing deep inside me to pushing me further and further away, though I wished I could erase every moment of that push and pull. She saw him kiss me gently, then look right through me, though it hurt to admit how much I still craved that closeness. My chest tightened with a mix of longing and resentment, though I forced myself to breathe through it.

Skylar sucked in a scant breath, though her hands didn't falter in their comforting rhythm. Ali, both amazed and confused, was putting the puzzle pieces together, though he struggled to grasp the full scope. Each subtle flicker of his expression stabbed me with the reminder that he didn't fully understand, though he was trying.

"She speaks to you... but through emotion?" he asked Skylar.

"I'm bound to her. She can't hide any part of herself from me," Skylar said, her voice heavier than the words themselves. The tether between us, unseen but undeniable, like a hand pressed to my chest, keeping me from drifting too far. A silent understanding that anchored me even as my thoughts swarmed.

Ali's eyes narrowed as he processed what Skylar said, though his confusion was plain. "So every emotion, every thought, she can't hide it from you?"

Skylar nodded slowly. "Not even the parts she tries to."

I swallowed hard, though the lump in my throat refused to move. "It's difficult," I admitted quietly. "Feeling everything, knowing someone else feels it too. It's exhausting, though it also keeps me from completely losing myself."

"Were you two… once lovers then?" Ali questioned. A whirlwind of wonder behind his eyes.

We both laughed. "No, you damn creep!" Skylar snapped at him, her hands still gentle in my hair. Men have to be one of God's simplest creations.

Ali raised his hands in mock surrender; confusion still colored his face. "What does it feel like?" he asked.

"Like breathing," Skylar answered.

Ali's eyes lingered on me, searching for a way to understand what he couldn't yet grasp. "This is unlike anything I've ever seen?"

"The fact that you are so present in this world, but still so blind to the wonders that it holds…is baffling," Skylar frowned. "Your grandmother must have shielded you from real magic, which has done you a disservice. Yet your brother is damn near the prince of darkness."

Ali's jaw tightened as he processed her words, his eyes searching mine. "I'm willing to learn."

Skylar's hands paused on my shoulders, her fingers pressed softly as she let out a quiet breath.

I guess now it was my turn to feel. Skylar's energy softened as she considered letting him deeper in. Her pulse slowed as the heat rose inside her.

She tested the water.

"I can show you," she teased.

With a lifted brow, "Show me what?" he asked.

She searched his face, lingering at his lips. "How it feels."

"Guy's, I'm still… right here, in my house." I interjected.

Ali smiled and playfully nudged my shoulder. "Okay, Sky and I will work on that lesson a little later. For now, you tell me what really happened tonight?"

"Your brother… went cold as ice…" my heart tightened around the words. "One moment I was his everything… now I'm… here. Back home,"

Sky froze for a moment, then said, "In this moment, you are exactly where you need to be." She squeezed my shoulders before getting up and heading into the kitchen.

Ali scooted beside me. His presence was soothing. His pale eyes glanced around his surroundings before he spoke. "You know, I knew you were special, but I can't say I knew exactly how. But your energy was… powerful."

I chuckled. "Ali, I watched you control a whole crowd with two turntables and one drum. Try that on for power."

He smiled. "My brother gave me that drum to show me that relics aren't all bad. Prior to that, I had only seen them weaponized. Sold to the highest bidder…families destroyed, innocent people controlled."

"That sounds weird coming from a protector," I added. "You're telling me people buy relics? What in the entire fuck?" I asked, both amazed and repulsed at the thought. Skylar returned, handing us each a glass before pouring bourbon into them. She placed the bottle on the coffee table and joined us.

"Ali was just saying that people actually buy relics." I said, still bothered by the idea.

"Yeah," Sky replied, The shock I had was absent in her expression. Then her expression changed from blank to dread. "Ali." Her tone was sharper. She shook her head vigorously now, as if she were trying to banish a thought. "No, no, no."

Ali's brow furrowed. "What is it?"

Skylar threw back the rest of her drink. She set her glass in her lap, fingers lingering on the rim as if bracing herself. Her eyes narrowed, scanning Ali's face, reading the unspoken history she'd only just pieced together. "Your family… y'all are fucking Crownbrokers?"

His eyes dropped to the ground. "I'm just a DJ, and a creative. I've never really been involved in what my family does. Eli made sure I was never involved," he admitted. "But I've seen some terrible things," he added.

"God, you don't know your real legacy… do you?" Skylar asked him.

"I've seen the lengths people will go to get the power of a relic. I've seen the horrible things some people do because of them. People will betray their own, steal from families, even kill… all for a chance to hold that kind of power. That's what my family does to live… but, Skylar, it's not my legacy."

Skylar directed her attention to me now. "Yani, you don't know what Crownbrokers are, do you?"

I shook my head, my stomach tightening.

"They're people who deal in relics," Skylar said, her voice low. "They buy them, sell them, trade them… whatever it takes. Some of them don't care who gets hurt. As long as the check clears."

She turned to Ali. "Your legacy is that you were born a protector.

That's why you can sense relics. But the woman that raised you, kept you from ever learning your true power."

Ali's gaze blurred as his eyes flooded with tears, and I could feel his confusion. He hadn't realized he had any power at all. Not the way Skylar described it, he never understood relics were more that products for distribution. For him, it had always been music, crowds, and rhythm. Now, in this quiet room, the weight of a legacy he had never been aware of was now crushing him alive.

I placed my hand on his shoulder. "Looks like we might both have a lot to learn."

******

By the time the night settled, exhaustion pulled at all of us. Ali had barely said another word before Skylar convinced him to lie down.

I sat on top of the island in my kitchen, drinking chamomile tea from my favorite cup. Skylar stepped in to join me before my thoughts wandered too far.

"He knocked the fuck out in the guest room; that valerian really did the trick. Thank you," she said as she leaned on the counter beside me.

"No problem," I replied, even though my hands were still trembling. "Punk," she smiled, playfully punching my thigh.

"Did you make enough for me?" She asked, pointing to my cup.

"Yours is in the microwave." She walked across the room to get it. When she returned, cup in hand, she blew lightly before taking a slow sip.

"You know, I know we both saw how that hit him. But only you can understand how he's feeling at this moment. Like his whole life has been a lie so far. "

I nodded. "I understand," I said, finally comprehending. To learn your life is a different tale than the one you believed you knew is a hard truth to bear." I looked away, pretending to focus on the steam rising from my tea. "But he'll figure it out. We all have to."

"But unlike you, he doesn't have someone on his side to put together the puzzle pieces."

"Like you said back at the lab, that woman had some weird shit going on…" I laughed into my cup."

"Says the woman with her ass sitting on the countertop!" Skylar shot back, grinning ear to ear.

I just rolled my eyes and continued sorting through this evening's chaos. "Ali seemed so heartbroken and confused," I added, remembering how my heart seized when I looked into his eyes.

"The heartbreak is just the beginning. Before I finally convinced him to rest, his anger had all but consumed him. From his grandmother, he wants answers. But with his brother though, he doest know whether he is sympathetic or furious. He wants to confront them both, and, like, right now," Skylar added.

"I'm certain he is not about to get any answers from her." I added as I thought back to the night at the Shell Joint. Those pale, guarded eyes were looking through me. Daring me to attempt entry.

"I'm sure tomorrow will be even more challenging. Shit, we might as well both have a little of that concoction you gave him too. Get a good night's sleep and deal with the rest tomorrow."

I sucked my teeth. "Girl, that stuff doesn't affect me anymore." Titi explained that as protectors, our DNA is coated with enhanced senses and an inherent need for alertness. "Valerian root, chamomile, melatonin. Delicious in my tea, but anything that would sedate me ultimately is just melted by my bloodline. Just another one of those quirks of being a protector."

Skylar's eyes widened; her cup almost froze at her lips. "Wait. If it doesn't work on Protectors…" Her voice trailed off as she sat down her cup and bolted for the hallway.

I followed directly behind her.

But when we reached the spare bedroom, Ali and his belongings were gone. The bedspread kept the lingering warmth of his body in the space he had occupied. All that remained was the smell of grief and confusion, a thick fog clinging to the space.

18

INFERNO
(Eli)

The moment I opened my eyes, I was greeted with the dread of yesterday. The air was stale, heavy with questions I didn't want to face. I'd spent all night trying to reach my brother, but nothing. Now, the weight of everything I knew pressed against my chest.

Everything I was had been forced on me. I had the world in my hands, but none of it mattered, not when I'd lost the one thing that meant the world to me.

Ayana.

And truth be told, she'd been right all along. She'd asked about the possibility of changing, and I shut her down without a thought. Now I saw she wasn't crazy for asking. The silence of her absence was piercing. I was used to her being here.

Even with the truth of yesterday still fresh, I had business at the warehouse that needed handling. Money couldn't stop moving over a broken heart or an identity crisis. If I didn't show up, I'd be sending the wrong message. No matter what, I was still the one in charge.

I pushed out of bed and forced myself to move. Routine would help. In the shower, I let the hot water wash some of the weight from me. Then lotion, black slacks, black shirt, Rolex. I slipped on my shoes and caught my reflection in the mirror across the room. Put together on the outside, wrecked underneath.

No way was I driving today. I paid a driver for a reason. Before I finished getting ready, I called Roderick to earn his keep.

******

Roderick navigated the road with quiet efficiency. I leaned back into the plush leather, head resting, mind trapped in the night before. The city blurred past the windows.

The closer we got to the warehouse, the tighter my chest became. Everything I'd built. Everything I controlled depended on my showing up like I owned it. No cracks. No weakness.

We crept to a halt under the gray haze of the Ash Zone. I stayed in the car longer than usual, letting the silence settle.

"All set, boss man," Roderick said from the driver's seat.

I pushed the door open and stepped into the darkness. Jay was nearby, idly flicking a gold lighter and staring into space. He looked up as I approached.

"You're l-l-l-late." His usual stutter was almost comforting.

"Yeah," I said, voice flat, not much weight behind it.

I headed toward my office, and he followed close behind. I sank into the oak desk chair, letting the weight of the night press down.

"Y-Y-You okay, man?" Jay asked, sinking into the loveseat along the nearest wall, eyes nervously on me.

"Man, I need a drink," I admitted, resting my elbows on the desk, head in my hands.

He walked over to the wet bar and poured two neat whiskeys, placing one in front of me and holding the other as he leaned against the desk.

"Whiskey before n-n-noon? Must be serious," he said, taking a sip.

I looked at him. "Jay, have you heard from my brother at all recently?"

"No, boss," he said, setting his glass down. "Not a peep."

I drained the rest of my whiskey and pushed back from the desk. "Shipment on time?"

"Like clockwork, boss. It's all handled."

Before I could say another word, a sudden angst enveloped me. The charm on my chest burned, and the fire behind my eyes poured out slowly. The room felt smaller now, like the shadow of yesterday was closing in.

"B-B-Boss, w-w-what's wrong?" Jay asked.

I didn't answer. I pushed to my feet and was halfway to the door when we both heard the crash.

The sound splintered through the warehouse. The earth shook beneath us. Then another crash. Louder, closer. Like the warehouse itself had taken a breath and shuddered.

Jay froze, eyes wide. "Th-th-that did not sound good."

I tightened my grip on the edge of the desk. The charm burned hotter, warning me of what I already knew. Someone or something was here.

I stepped onto the main floor of the warehouse, and far down the walkway lined with crates, he stood.

My twin brother.

A pulse ran up my chest. The charm on my neck choked out a silent scream. Movement followed, deliberate, heavy, unstoppable.

Jay froze behind me. I didn't need words. My blood already knew before my eyes confirmed it.

There he was, framed by crates and shadow.

My twin.

Roderick came rushing in from outside and froze when he saw Ali moving toward us.

As he walked, Ali gripped the sides of crates, ripping them loose and tossing their contents across the floor. The same wild look burned in his eyes as it had the day before. A fury.

"Haze," Roderick muttered. "He's on Haze… and a lot of it, boss."

"Ali," I said, my voice cracking before I could clear my throat. My heart broke looking into his vacant stare, his gray, ashen skin cracking before my eyes. "I've been trying to reach you, bro. What did you do?"

Ali's voice hit like a thunderclap. "What did I do? Me? What did *you* do?" He stepped closer, shaking. "I know you're behind the missing girls. You fucking monster! And I set them all free!"

Ali's voice literally caused the room to shake.

The punch behind the last syllable slammed Roderick and Jay against the wall.

His chest heaved, violent and unevenly, like his ribs might tear apart. His body jolted. Then, with a strength that didn't belong to any man, he tore another crate in half, splinters and dust exploding through the air.

"Ali!" I shouted.

Slowly, his head turned, but his eyes didn't find me. His pupils were gone, clouded white by the Haze burning through his veins.

Roderick and Jay drew their weapons and advanced.

"No!" The word ripped from my throat, raw and primal. The relic around my neck seared against my skin, fire crawling up my chest. Fear and rage collided until I couldn't tell them apart.

Ali lunged, crashing into me with enough force to rattle my ribs. The floor shook beneath us.

Jay and Roderick stood frozen, uncertain. The creature that used to be my brother pinned me to the ground.

"Go!" I barked.

They hesitated, then backed up together, disappearing through the front door.

With all the strength I had left, I threw Ali off me, his body crashing into a stack of crates. I scrambled to my feet, chest heaving.

"The fuck is wrong with you, Ali?" I shouted. "I spent my whole life protecting yours. You've never had to work for anything. I opened the club so you'd never have to live this life. When we were kids, I took every beating meant for you. Now you show up here, destroying everything I've built. For what? You ungrateful bastard. We were both lied to."

Ali's laugh cracked through the air, high and broken. "But you became the lie, Eli. A puppet, who doesn't even need fucking strings anymore."

He grabbed a crate and hurled it. It smashed against the wall beside me, raining splinters across the floor. The air around me was a cloud of dust and ash.

"And you got to entertain the world," I shouted almost in tears, "while I held this family together on my fucking back!"

Ali, fully crazed, charged at me full force, ramming his shoulder into my chest. I stumbled to the wall behind me. The impact rattled through my spine. I barely had time to bring my arms up before his fist connected with my jaw. My face whipped to the right as I dug into the wall to keep myself upright. I caught his arm as his fists attempted to rain down once more, locking his wrists and pushing back with everything I had.

"Ali, stop!" I yelled, straining against him. His skin burned hot beneath my grip, veins dark and pulsing with haze. "It's me, man. You're not thinking straight."

He snarled, twisting free with impossible strength. The smell of ash and sweat filled the air. Ali charged again before I could steady myself.

His hand clamped around my throat and slammed me back into the concrete wall.

The impact sent my skull crashing into the concrete. My lungs were struggling to move air as I attempted to pry his hands away from me.

His grip only tightened.

His eyes, a blur of white, looked through me. Haze surged through him like static.

I planted my feet and propelled myself forward, slamming my chest into his. Ali stumbled back, crashing against the concrete floor further down the hall with a grunt. Dust rose around him as he struggled to regain his balance, and for a brief second, I could breathe.

Now my necklace felt as if it was taking on a life of its own. It pulsed like a live heartbeat. The warmth from my chest spread then with a gust. Flames crawled along the edges of the crates that lined the walls around us, circling us seductively, prowling the room.

They weren't just bright light. They were alive, were aware, hungry, teasing, licking at the concrete and my skin with seductive strokes. I felt it whispering, urging me, daring me to let it loose.

The fire curled along the perimeter like a graceful lioness circling her prey. Leaning closer to me, licking the air with a sultry hiss, sparks drifting upward like the flicker of her lashes.

Her heat was pure passion, pressing against my skin, testing my limits, whispering the want for more. I could feel her, the fire, measuring us both.

I lunged at Ali as he charged, catching his shoulder and twisting him just enough to throw him off balance. He slammed onto the concrete floor, grunting as dust rose around him. Fists and elbows met bone and muscle, every strike echoing in the cavernous warehouse. The fire swirled along the crates and floor, brushing against us, daring and alive, testing the limits of our bodies and our rage.

Ali's eyes locked on the flames, a sudden break in his frenzy, and then he looked back to me.

In that moment, we remembered.

We knew this fire.

We knew her very well.

She's curled around him, teasing, daring him to strike.

Ali did not resist. With a jarring roar, he sprang forward, the concrete quaking beneath his weight, his fists swinging wild. The flames danced around him, brushing his shoulders as he moved.

Ali lunged again, fists aiming for my head and ribs in a relentless blur. I ducked his wild advances. Then, when he lost balance, I twisted my torso to slam my shoulder into his midsection. He staggered, but didn't fall, his strength still powered by the high.

Sweat and ash mixed in the air as we collided. My fists found his shoulders; his elbows slammed into my ribs. Every strike sent sparks flickering along the crates, her flames dancing higher with every hit. She was teasing, daring us both, pushing us toward something dangerous.

The fire curled higher, hips swaying side to side, licking along the crates and floor, framing the two of us.

It didn't burn.

Not yet.

It watched, coaxing, daring, prodding us both toward the edge.

I grabbed my brother by the wrist, halting his wild swings, restraining him as he cursed and spat like a possessed beast.

I planted my feet firmly and hurled my brother further down the hall.

Now the monster inside was daring to take over. I prowled along the embers, and she pressed against the walls. I could feel her temper rising now.

I gave in to the fire that lived behind my eyes. Releasing my fury with each step.

Ali lunged.

I Advanced.

We sparred through the flames as we exchanged punches, propelled by more power than the blows that preceded them.

The fire grew angrier, higher, hotter.

She roared as we clashed against each other.

Then, with my hand around his throat, he struggled to pry away my grip.

Her temper rose higher, flames gathering to the left of me in a wrenching roar.

Ali was getting weaker.

I was over the edge. Feeding off of raw anger.

She nudged me now.

She was something beautiful.

Something terrible.

Calling me over the edge.

And what did I have to lose? The fire had reached its peak, curling like a living thing, roaring, clawing at the air.

I felt it pressing against my skin, daring me to go further, to give it everything. Then, with one last surge of strength, I released my brother, ripped the charm from my neck and flung it into her hungry blaze.

Then, just as fast as she had arrived, the fire was gone.

The air stilled. For a moment, everything was quiet except for the sound of my heart pounding in my chest, but different somehow.

Wilder, unrestrained for the first time in years.

My hand went to the empty space on my chest where the charm had hung. The skin felt raw, tender, like a wound finally exposed to air.

Jay and Roderick ran inside to my rescue, and my brother dropped to the ground. He was alive, but barely conscious.

I kneeled beside him, touching his face. The same face as mine, yet so different now. Something broke between us.

Something that had been draining him while anchoring me.

He needed help.

I knew only one place to go. But as I gathered Ali in my arms, I could already feel it. Something unleashed inside me, something I'd never had to face without the charm's restraint.

Whatever came next, I would face it changed. Whatever power I'd held before was nothing compared to what might follow.

For Ali, it was worth the risk.

19

FIRE'S CALL

(Yah-Yah)

"Where do y'all think this child would even go?" Titi asked, genuine concern beneath her usual snappy tone.

Fresh coffee filled the air in my living room, where the three of us sat gathered. Skylar had called Titi after she'd run out of options. Of course, Titi reminded us we should've called her before we even got into this mess.

"Shit, y'all sure can pick 'em." She laughed from her gut. "Well, someone pour Auntie something stronger while we figure a way through this madness. It won't hold, but it'll take the edge off."

I rubbed my temples. She was supposed to be making this better. I grabbed wine glasses from the kitchen while Skylar went to the cellar for a bottle.

"When he start shacking up over here anyway? I thought Skylar and Mark were working on working things out."

"And who the hell told you that?" Skylar entered, bottle in hand.

"Hell?!" Titi snapped. "I see you went down them stairs and bumped your head on the way back up here, huh?"

"No, ma'am," Skylar said softly.

"And when did you even get back home, chile? I thought you went to be with your man?" The interrogation turned to me. "You and him...I've seen nothing like it," Titi whispered. "It's like watching two magnets that can't help but snap together. Dangerous, maybe, but there's something... destined about it."

Skylar poured wine into our glasses, her hands shaking.

I sank into the sofa, letting out a long breath. How had this become my reality? Last week, things felt perfect. Last week I had the love of my life. What happened to my happily ever after?

My thoughts stopped because of a furious knock on the door. The sound shook through the room.

I ran to find Roderick, Eli's driver, on the other side. He opened his mouth to speak, but my eyes caught past him. Eli was coming up the steps, carrying a barely conscious Ali in his arms.

"Boss lady, can you take care of them? I wasn't sure where else to take them," Roderick said.

He turned to leave, but I caught his arm. "No, stay. You're family too." I said before I called back to the living room, "Umm, Titi?"

Then, with no warning, Eli crossed the threshold, bringing Ali to the sofa.

My mouth dropped.

Titi and Skylar rushed to help while I stood frozen.

They were both disheveled and beaten, clothes torn, bodies marked by soot and blood. And Eli.

Standing there in my living room.

The charm on his neck was gone.

His chest bare, bruised, streaked with ash and sweat.

Just Eli.

"You're here," I whispered.

"I'm here," he said, pulling me close. My chest tightened.

He tilted my chin, and our lips met. I wrapped my arms around his neck, lost in the warmth of him. His hands steadied me, grounding me.

For a moment, the world disappeared.

Then, a harsh sound broke through. Ali's breath rasped low, uneven, too thin.

"Ahem." Skylar's voice trembled. "I don't mean to interrupt, but..."

"I need to know what went wrong so I can make it right," Titi said from the sofa, Ali limp across her lap.

Eli pulled away and moved to his brother's side. Kneeling, he hesitated.

"He showed up at my warehouse high on haze. Wild. Feral. Then the fire came out of nowhere," he said, voice rough. "We—we were—"

"That's what I need to know," Titi cut in, firm and calm. "Now move back and let Sky in here so she can tell me the rest."

Eli obeyed. Titi pressed her palms to Ali's temples, voice low and sure. The air hummed, a gentle whisper that grew into a powerful vibration, as though the room itself was inhaling. Ali's color slowly returned.

When Titi looked up, the whites of her eyes were gone, replaced by endless black. The language that spilled from her lips sounded ancient, like the earth itself was speaking through her.

Skylar pressed her palms to Ali's chest, her face tightening as if she felt his pain through her own body. Tears streamed freely down her cheeks.

A strange heaviness filled my chest. My knees buckled, and before I could fall, Eli caught me, steadying me in his arms.

"You good, babe?" he asked softly.

I simply answered him with a nod. Then my curiosity wouldn't let me hold back any longer.

"Eli?" I asked softly. "What about the girls? The girls that were missing."

His head and shoulders dropped. "Well, my jackass of a brother set them all free not understanding that most of them I was protecting there. Some of them had unfair bounties on their heads," Eli added as I gasped. "Jay is making sure they get to the authorities as we speak. No more secrets." His gaze dropped to my sternum, and his brow furrowed. "Whoa. When did you get this tattoo?"

I looked down. The compass on my skin glowed faintly, pulsing in rhythm with my heartbeat.

I laughed, pulling him closer to me. "Long story." I caught his gaze. Those eyes still mesmerized me.

"Well, lucky for you, I've got all the time in the world," he said, his voice low, eyes warm. The edges of his smile spread slowly before a heavy grunt from the sofa pulled our attention back.

Ali stirred, a low groan escaping his throat. His fingers twitched, then his chest lifted with a sharp, shuddering breath. The air in the room shifted, lighter somehow. When his eyes opened, confusion flickered there, then softened into recognition. "Eli?"

Eli rushed to him, pulling him into a fierce embrace. "Baby brother." He pressed a kiss to his brow, nearly crushing him in his arms.

Ali's hand rested on his brother's bare chest, his gaze catching where the charm would have been. His eyes widened in disbelief before he pulled his brother into another embrace. Then, like clockwork, when they separated, their hands kept moving in sync, fists connecting, thumbs interlocking, wings fluttering between them.

20

NEW FLAME

(ELI)

The sun shone down on my face as a light breeze danced across my skin.

New.

Refreshing.

I hadn't intended to be a tagalong today, but something had pulled me here. Surrounded by a mix of cobblestone and green space, I inhaled the scent of fresh roses and the faint aroma of baked goods from nearby stalls.

I reached out and touched the flowers at the wooden booth in front of me. Their petals were soft in my hand, despite my rough grip. My world was clearly changing. The air didn't feel heavy anymore.

From somewhere nearby, a violin sang softly, its notes drifting over the chatter of vendors and the laughter of children. I focused ahead, squinting against the bright beam of sun above.

A sudden thud hit my right foot, and I winced. "Ahh!!" Looking down, I saw a little girl with a small toy grocery cart had rammed right into me. Not too long ago, this might have set me off. Now I just smiled. Her bright, tear-filled eyes stared up at me as her upside-down grin quivered. The impact had knocked the contents of her cart sprawling across the cobblestones.

I kneeled to meet her at eye level. "Now what's got you crying like that, little mama?" I asked, picking up the plastic food replicas and placing them back inside her cart. "See, nothing to cry for. All is well again." I handed it to her.

Her face lit up. She beamed and rolled away, laughter trailing behind her like wind chimes caught in a summer breeze.

When I stood, Skylar was right in front of me. Her signature bright green headphones, no longer present. Her smile was brighter than usual, almost glowing, and for a moment I could see the calm I felt reflected at me.

"Boy, what are you doing? Got us walking up here all alone; you're the one that wanted to come with us," she said, rolling her eyes playfully.

I brushed her off with a laugh, keeping my focus beyond her until I could find my target.

Then I saw her.

Just like that, all the surrounding noise faded.

Ayana.

The breeze shifted her hair across her face, and she looked back at me with the same quiet smile. She reached for a basket of fruit, her hand resting lightly on her lower back to support her pregnant belly. For once, I didn't feel fire. I felt warmth.

I noticed the gentle sway of her movements, the way she took careful steps on the cobblestones, and something in me relaxed entirely. This simple moment was worth more than anything I had fought for before.

When we left, Ayana and I would return to the brownstone in Royal Hills, the one we had been remodeling and preparing for the new edition of our life. Skylar would head back to the penthouse she now shared with my twin brother, a home filled with laughter and love.

And as for my old apartment, Titi and the girls had completely taken it over, converting it into a second state-of-the-art lab and relic vault.

I inhaled the scent of roses once more, letting the sun warm me. The world felt alive. And maybe, just maybe, it was finally ours.

Epilogue

And there you have it.

An unexpected ending with an unlikely antagonist. But for my grandson's success in this story, I will gladly play the villain in theirs.

One thing though is for sure. This story's origin differs drastically from the depiction here. If only I had paid closer attention to the girl's full surname. I focused too much on her surname being Broussard. I ignored the weight of her being also named Caroll.

The Caroll family once held the Bone Torch of Nakia. Its power had mistakenly started the Great Fire of Nevermore. A ritual intended to rid the city of evil and restore purity ended with a mistake that spread the fire uncontrollably.

In Haiti, the fire from that same relic killed my husband when he tried to harness its power. Years later, it returned and claimed my son, reducing my home to ash. I watched it all happen with no one to save me, no one to grieve with.

My grandson and Ayana, seemingly fulfilling a prophecy, would together restore Nevermore to the place it once was.

Quietly, I wait, allowing the embers of the past to smolder until I claim what is owed.